# TOP-

*He's not just the boss, he's the best...*

These heroes aren't just doctors, they're life-savers.

These heroes aren't just surgeons, they're skilled masters. Their talent and reputation are admired by all.

These heroes are devoted to their patients.
They'll hold the littlest babies in their arms,
and melt the hearts of all who see.

These heroes aren't just medical professionals.
They're the men of your dreams.

*He's not just the boss, he's the best there is!*

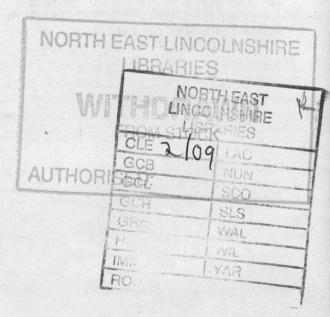

NORTH EAST LINCOLNSHIRE
LIBRARIES

WITHDRAWN
FROM STOCK

AUTHORISED

| NORTH EAST LINCOLNSHIRE LIBRARIES | | |
|---|---|---|
| CLE | 2/09 | LAC |
| GCB | | NUN |
| GCL | | SCO |
| GCR | | SLS |
| GRA | | WAL |
| H | | WIL |
| IMM | | YAR |
| RO | | |

Now that her children have left home, **Dianne Drake** is finally finding the time to do some of the things she adores—gardening, cooking, reading, shopping for antiques. Her absolute passion in life, however, is adopting abandoned and abused animals. Right now Dianne and her husband Joel have a little menagerie of three dogs and two cats, but that's always subject to change. A former symphony orchestra member, Dianne now attends the symphony as a spectator several times a month and, when time permits, takes in an occasional football, basketball or hockey game.

# A BOSS
# BEYOND COMPARE

BY
DIANNE DRAKE

**MILLS & BOON**
*Pure reading pleasure™*

**DID YOU PURCHASE THIS BOOK WITHOUT A COVER?**

If you did, you should be aware it is **stolen property** as it was reported *unsold and destroyed* by a retailer. Neither the author nor the publisher has received any payment for this book.

All the characters in this book have no existence outside the imagination of the author, and have no relation whatsoever to anyone bearing the same name or names. They are not even distantly inspired by any individual known or unknown to the author, and all the incidents are pure invention.

All Rights Reserved including the right of reproduction in whole or in part in any form. This edition is published by arrangement with Harlequin Enterprises II BV/S.à.r.l. The text of this publication or any part thereof may not be reproduced or transmitted in any form or by any means, electronic or mechanical, including photocopying, recording, storage in an information retrieval system, or otherwise, without the written permission of the publisher.

This book is sold subject to the condition that it shall not, by way of trade or otherwise, be lent, resold, hired out or otherwise circulated without the prior consent of the publisher in any form of binding or cover other than that in which it is published and without a similar condition including this condition being imposed on the subsequent purchaser.

® and TM are trademarks owned and used by the trademark owner and/or its licensee. Trademarks marked with ® are registered with the United Kingdom Patent Office and/or the Office for Harmonisation in the Internal Market and in other countries.

First published in Great Britain 2008
Harlequin Mills & Boon Limited,
Eton House, 18-24 Paradise Road, Richmond, Surrey TW9 1SR

© Dianne Despain 2008

ISBN: 978 0 263 86354 3

Set in Times Roman 10¼ on 12¾ pt
03-1008-56863

Printed and bound in Spain
by Litografia Rosés, S.A., Barcelona

# A BOSS
# BEYOND COMPARE

| NORTH EAST LINCOLNSHIRE COUNCIL | |
|---|---|
| 00913371 | |
| Bertrams | 23/01/2009 |
| R | £2.99 |
| | |

# CHAPTER ONE

"YOU can't just walk out like this!" Walter Ridgeway stepped away from the end of the conference table where, only minutes before, he'd just merged two small medical facilities into one larger one. He walked toward his daughter. "We've got too many things going on right now, and I need you here."

"I'm not just walking out," Susan said, on a weary sigh. "And you don't need me here right now. You just want me here because you need someone to bully." That was said affectionately. Her father really didn't bully her, but he was demanding, used to getting his way.

"So what's wrong with having my daughter by my side? We're a team, Susan. I depend on you."

She laughed. He was so good at the art of negotiation, yet he was failing miserably here. And he knew that. Yet he didn't give up, which was what made Walter Ridgeway so successful at what he did. No matter what the situation, he went at it to win. "You depend on yourself and nobody else, Dad. But you're right, we are a team, and this half of the team needs a holiday." It was overdue. In fact, the last real holiday she'd had had been, what? Nineteen years ago? She'd been fifteen and her father had taken her away to Switzerland to ski. Of course, it had been a business trip, too. For him, it had always been a business trip.

But that week in Switzerland had been the last time she'd had any kind of a holiday, and having one now wasn't just overdue. It was long overdue. "Dr O'Brien told me that if I don't take a little downtime he's going to put me on stress pills." Her father was a doctor, she was a doctor, yet for her medical care she still relied on the kindly near-octogenarian who'd been her doctor all her life. It galled her father a bit, seeing that Ridgeway Medical employed some of the best doctors in the world, but there was something nice about going to a doctor who knew her, one who cared. It was a personal kind of medicine she didn't get to direct in her capacity as chief medical officer for Ridgeway Medical, which was why she hung on to Dr O'Brien so fiercely, even though he was in semi-retirement. For Susan, the old family practitioner was like a cozy warm blanket and a good, hot cup of tea. Comfort items, all of them. "So, I'm going to follow doctor's orders and take a holiday."

"After the Hawaii deal is sealed. Then you can have all the time you need."

Ah, the same old story. She knew he meant it when he said it, but it never came to pass. Which was the problem. She didn't thrive on tension and having every last nerve ending in her body stretched to snapping point, the way her father did. He not only thrived on it, he invited it—the more the merrier. But her temperament was a bit more subdued. "Which is what you said after the Atlanta deal, and after the Chicago deal. Now here I am, still no holiday and it's three years later. I need to go, Dad. Just for a few days." She had some thinking to do and she needed time and space to do it.

Stopping three feet short of his daughter, Walter crossed his arms over his chest. There was no give in his expression. Glowering all the way. So much so, anyone looking on would not have been able to tell that this was a father looking at his daughter. "You *can* be replaced," he warned.

This was the same argument he'd used last time she'd wanted a few days away. Only this time it wasn't going to work. He was a formidable man, but she had her own amount of formidability, too. "If that's what you want to do…" Susan shrugged casually. "Then do it." He wouldn't, of course. And he knew that she knew he would not. But this was just part of the relationship, part of the long-standing dynamic they had going between them. Her father was a controlling man, and he was used to getting his way.

Today wasn't going to be his day, though.

Taking in a deep breath, Susan took those three steps that separated them, kissed her father on the cheek, then walked out of the office, and out of the building, without a notion in the world of where she was going, or what she was going to do for the next ten days.

Grant Makela caught sight of her. This was the third morning she'd come to the beach. Same time, same spot, same stupid hat.

He'd noticed her that first morning, picking up shells. Pathetic little shells, broken bits and pieces. Yet she'd seemed so delighted by them. Almost like a child finding a treasure. He'd really hoped she would find something good washed ashore, but that rarely happened on this beach.

So the next morning, for whatever reason he still couldn't explain, he'd bought a little mesh bag of shells from one of the local souvenir dealers, and dumped them in a pile near the spot where she'd been sitting the day before, hoping she'd return.

She did come back, and when she found those shells she scooped them right into her pockets. She was a woman who was thrilled with a simple prize, and she didn't question anything about it. That showed an innocence Grant found appealing. At a time in his life when so many things were going wrong, that was nice. Even if only for a few moments in the morning.

"Don't do it," he muttered to himself, as he prepared to take his first wave of the day. "Don't even think about getting involved with her." No time, no interest… He was about to say no sex drive either, but that wasn't the case. It was there. Just not so noticeable these days.

Turning back to the surf, Dr Etana Grant Makela kicked his sandals into the sand and took his first steps into the water. Three. That's what he'd allow himself this morning. Three waves, then he had patients to see.

Her surfer had left the beach an hour ago, same surfboard tucked under his right arm, same bold strides across the sand she'd watched for three days. And now she was impatient to leave, too. Impatient, like her father, which was exactly why she didn't get up and walk away. She was on holiday now. The one she'd fought for. She'd walked out the door, gone straight to the airport and come to Hawaii, since this was the site of their next meeting anyway. Yet, as much as she hated to admit it, the impatience with so much leisure time was beginning to trickle in. "Read a book, take a nap," she said aloud, as a reminder. "Watch the surfers." Even though not one of them held the same appeal as the surfer Adonis she watched every morning. He was perfection, and the rest were…unremarkable.

A group of five young boys running toward the water, all with surfboards tucked under their arms, did catch Susan's attention for a moment, though. They were having so much fun. Young, probably college-aged, all of them taking a break, doing some surfing, looking at the pretty girls, probably drinking too much, sleeping too little. The follies of youth, she supposed, picking up her book and hunting for the page where she'd left off.

The follies of anything, that's what she missed. That had been part of her confusion lately, and the whole reason why she'd come on holiday. There were things to think about, life decisions to make. Turning her attention to the book, Susan was staring at the page more than reading it, when, suddenly, something in the distance caught her attention. A number of people on the beach were running toward…well, she couldn't make it out, but she could hear the far-off shouts, could see more and more people moving in that direction. Then people were huddling about something, and screaming.

The warning hairs on the back of her neck suddenly prickling, Susan jumped up, dropping her paperback into the sand, and started off toward the gathering group, which was growing larger by the moment. A few moderate steps, followed by a few faster ones, then she broke into a full run, her bare feet burned by the hot sand as she fought through the growing group, shoving herself to the front of it, where she nearly stumbled over a young man, probably not more than twenty years old, sprawled on his back. Mullet haircut, cartoon-character tattoos on his chest, he wasn't moving.

Without a thought about it, her true nature took over. "Stand back," she shouted, dropping to her knees next to the boy. "I'm a doctor." Magic words. Everybody stepped back and the noisy crowd hushed, except for another young man who appeared to be the same age as the one in distress. Normal brown hair, no tattoos.

"Do something!" he cried. "You gotta do something."

Susan did. She began an assessment of the boy in the sand. First discovery—no pulse.

"Board came back up and hit him," the other young man said. "He couldn't have seen it coming."

Second discovery—no respirations.

"He went under, but he didn't come back up right away. I went under looking for him."

Third discovery—blue lips, ashen pallor, pupils unresponsive.

*Time to perform CPR.* "How long?" she asked her patient's buddy.

"Huh?"

"How long was he under? How long ago did he stop breathing?"

"He's not breathing?" the buddy sputtered.

"How long?" Susan shouted, trying to get through to him. "Tell me how long?"

"I don't know. Maybe four or five minutes."

He was right on the cusp of either living or dying and could so easily tip one way or another, she thought as she did a quick exam of his neck. Surfboard injury could mean head trauma or even a broken neck. She couldn't move him if his neck was broken. "No more than that?"

"Uh, I don't know. Could have been. I wasn't really paying attention."

She nodded, not satisfied with the answer. But wasting more time asking was futile.

Gently, she probed one side of the young man's neck, then the other. Nothing visible, nothing to feel. No air moving in or out. No pain response to her sternal rub either.

Susan felt the boy tipping toward death, and she dragged in a shaky breath to steady herself. "We need to roll him over," she said, bracing her hands to splint his neck. She needed the water to drain from his mouth so she could begin resuscitation. Yet she had to pay attention to positioning his body, in case there was a serious spinal injury. A wrong move could make him a paraplegic or a quadriplegic.

"Don't over-think," she whispered. *No time to think. No time to weigh the options.*

She gestured to three men standing in the crowd, watching. "You, you and you…I need you to help me get him over on his side. Slowly." She pointed to the positioning she wanted from the men, then continued, "On the count of three, roll him gently onto his left side. No sudden movements, and don't jerk him." Brave words for what she was beginning to think the outcome might be, given all the options. But he was dead already as it was, and without moving him she couldn't perform CPR.

That was always the dilemma—to risk further, possibly permanent injury to save a life. Something, in all her years of being a doctor, she'd never had to deal with. Something she'd never had to put to the test until this very moment, as she braced the boy's neck with her hands, desperately wishing she'd had more experience in direct patient care. "One, two, three…"

In unison, the men moved the boy to his side and a substantial trickle of water drained from his mouth. But he didn't begin to breathe on his own, sputter a bit of it out and gasp for a re-placement of air, as she'd hoped he might. That did happen. Drain the water and spontaneous respirations began. But they hadn't, and a huge thorn of dread jabbed her spine. "Okay, roll him back over, same way," she instructed. "One, two, three…"

As the youth went back into the supine position, it was becoming obvious to the crowd watching on that they were losing ground. Time was almost gone.

Not to be daunted, however, Susan felt for a pulse in the boy's neck…still nothing. Then the pulse in his groin artery. Nothing again. Absolutely nothing.

The full knowledge was assaulting her now. It was too long. He was probably already past the point of return, too long without oxygen, but, still, it could happen, couldn't it? She'd read medical accounts of these situations, where better results were recorded. It might not be too late. It just couldn't be…

Susan started chest compressions and prepared to do mouth-to-mouth breathing, too, when a stranger emerged from the crowd and took over that duty. For the next several minutes, the two of them performed CPR quietly and skillfully. It was a frantic scene in which the crowd had stepped even farther back and a few people who didn't want to watch the final outcome had skittered away. No one standing around Susan and the stranger spoke either, no one moved. Susan almost wished they would make some noise, something to cover up the stark sound of silent death settling in, because with every chest compression that failed to produce a heartbeat, and with every breath the man across from her put into the boy that failed to draw out one of his own, her optimism diminished.

After five minutes of this, her arms were aching and burning, on the way to going numb. And nothing was happening.

But he was so young…too young to die. Somebody loved this boy…his mother, his father. A girlfriend waiting at home for him, making dreamy plans for their future. For the people who loved him, she wouldn't quit.

But she knew the rules. Ten to fifteen minutes without any response whatsoever meant it was hopeless. In her heart she did know this young man wasn't going to be resuscitated—her first patient in so many years she couldn't even remember, and she could not save him.

Yet she still couldn't quit. She looked plaintively at the man across from her, who was busy feeling for a pulse, and couldn't read his face. Maybe, like her, he was hoping that with the next compression of the boy's chest…maybe one more breath…maybe a miracle. Please, God, a miracle! "Don't do this," she whispered, as she continued to work frantically on the lifeless body. "Don't die." Empty words, but as long as she kept saying them there was hope. "Don't die…"

"It's time," the stranger finally said. He reached across the body and laid a gentle hand on her arm. "We've done every-thing we can do. It's time."

This was her resuscitation, not his! He didn't have the right to call it done. "Leave me alone!" she choked, shrug-ging off his touch.

"It's been too long. You can't save him."

"Go to hell," she snarled, continuing the chest compres-sions with a newfound strength and preparing herself to take over the rescue-breathing the stranger wasn't going to do, as he was moving away now.

"You tried, but he was under too long from the start." Behind her now, the stranger tried to take hold of her shoulders and pull her away, but she flailed out, struck him, and bent back over the boy for a round of mouth-to-mouth. Tears were streaking down her cheeks now. And her own breaths were coming in sobs.

"It's not too late!" she cried, going back to her chest com-pression position once she'd delivered the breaths. But this time the stranger succeeded in grabbing her, pulling her firmly away from the lifeless form, as someone from the crowd stepped forward and covered the boy with a beach blanket.

Susan still fought the man who held her back, though. Tried to get away from him, tried to get back to her patient. But the man held her away, held her tight. Pulled her into his arms and locked her there in his grip.

"It's time," he said, his voice so quiet it wasn't even a whisper. "I'm sorry, but there's nothing you can do for him now. He's dead, and he can't be resuscitated."

He was right. She knew that. *The doctor in her knew that.* There wasn't anything to be done now. The boy really was...

A sob so heavy it racked her entire body caused her to go limp in the man's arms, and she was grateful for the strength in his embrace, and for the gentleness, even if from a stranger.

She needed it. Needed something to hold on to. Needed some-one to hold on to her.

Susan laid her head on the stranger's chest and shut her eyes, listening to the sound of his beating heart, listening to the strength and vitality in it, taking comfort in the life she could hear, could feel against her cheek. "I tried," she said, sudden heavy lethargy washing down over her. She was so tired now. Exhausted with a bone-crushing weariness like she'd never known in her life. "I tried to save him." To her own ears her voice was thick, distorted.

"I know you did. But this wasn't your fault." He stroked her hair with the gentle hand of someone who cared. Of course, she knew he didn't. He was merely a stranger on the beach, doing what any compassionate stranger might do. But she was glad for his attention anyway, and craved it for a moment longer.

"Someone needs to notify—"

"Shh. It's not for you to worry about now. You did every-thing you could."

Easy for him to say, because he hadn't been the one who'd failed at the resuscitation attempt. He hadn't been the one to let the boy die. She was the one who had started it and she was the one who'd failed. Which made this man's need to calm her seem so…trivial. She didn't want his compassion any longer. Didn't want his arms around her any more, so she pushed herself away from him. "Don't you think you're taking this whole thing rather lightly?" she choked, pointing to the boy's body. "He just died, for God's sake! And you're behaving like…like…" She steadied herself with a deep breath. "I need to see the local doctor and find out if I need to sign the death certificate since I'm the one who…" Who'd let him die. She couldn't say the words out loud, though.

"Three blocks. That way." He pointed in the direction leading away from the beach. "White building. South side of the road. You can't miss it."

She thought about thanking the man for his comfort but didn't as he disappeared into the crowd when she took her last look at the boy. However it worked out from here, this definitely marked the end of her holiday.

# CHAPTER TWO

"YOU!"

From his desk, Grant Makela smiled up at Susan. "Are you feeling better?"

"What are you doing here?"

"You said you had to come see the local doctor about a death certificate, so here I am, the local doctor."

"Couldn't you have told me that on the beach?"

"Would you have heard me if I had? You were pretty upset."

"Were? I still am." A lump as hard as the slick volcanic pahoehoe stone she'd found on her walk to the beach that morning grabbed Susan by the throat, threatening to choke her. She swallowed hard, willing the anxiety to dissipate, willing the memories of that frightful scene to break up and go away. Yet the more she tried to not think about it, the more she did. All the while, that abominable lump in her throat was enlarging to the point it hurt. And the tears starting to slide down her cheeks felt like drops of molten lava burning a sharp path from her eyes straight to her heart as she thought of how someone who'd loved that young man must have been crying the same bitter, stinging tears for him, too.

Of all the times to be silly, here she was, doing it in front of him. Dr Makela, according to the nameplate on his desk. "I, um… Could I just sign whatever I need to, so I can go back to my hotel?"

"You're not driving, are you? Because I'm not sure you're in any shape to drive so soon."

She nodded, almost to the point of biting her inner lip to stop her emotions from gushing over.

"Well, maybe you should have a rest here before you go. Take a little time to calm down."

"I'm fine," she argued. "Just a bit…upset, like I said."

"No," he said in such a soft-spoken voice it caused her to shiver—the voice he'd used to comfort her on the beach.

It was amazing how quickly she'd come to like that voice, come to believe it.

"You're not fine. And upset is an understatement for what you're going through, judging by what I'm seeing. What happened out there…it's not an easy thing. And what you tried to do…your after-effects are natural, and I'd really like for you to stay until you've had time to get over it, to recover."

He did have a nice way about him, and she thought he was probably genuine in his concern, but right then she didn't want concern. All she wanted was to be alone. "I'm a doctor. I know very well what I am."

Dr Makela gave her a compassionate, patient smile. "I'm also a doctor, and I know very well what you are, too. You're feeling like emotional hell. Your hands are shaking, your head is probably woozy and pounding like crazy, and you hate me at this very moment because you'd rather go off to yourself and have a good cry, and I'm not letting you do that. Am I right about that?"

"The papers, Doctor? I know there are papers to sign so please, just let me do that, then you won't have to waste your time diagnosing someone who doesn't want to be diagnosed."

"But you do need to be diagnosed, Doctor…" He waited for her to divulge her name.

"Cantwell. Dr Susan Cantwell."

"Medical doctor?"

In a manner of speaking, yes, as that's the way she'd been trained. Technically, she was an internal medicine specialist. She also had a little background in general surgery, too. Both had been prerequisites for her position as medical director over any number of internists and surgeons. But here, after her failure, it seemed like such a bitter pill to swallow, admitting that she was a medical doctor. "Medical doctor," she said almost under her breath.

"A medical doctor who's not feeling so well right now. Would you like to go lie down for a while? I have a private room empty, and maybe after a little rest…"

"Apart from the humiliation at showing just how bad my skills are, Dr Makela, I'm just dandy!" she snapped. "Thank you for the offer, but I'm not in the mood for medical attention or sympathy right now."

"I can't say that I blame you. But you're not in any shape to drive yet, and unless you want to go back to the beach and rest there for a while, you're going to have to stay here, in the room I offered. I'd be remiss in my duties here if I allowed you to do anything else." He gave her a straight-on, provocative stare. "And I'm never remiss."

He was a little more insistent this time, his voice taking on a little harder edge. Forceful words, yet kind. Sexy eyes staring right through her. He was right about it, of course. She was in no shape to drive and she knew that. Her hands were shaking so hard she doubted she could even insert the key into the ignition. Just look at her! One failed resuscitation and she was a total wreck. Did he wonder about her emotional stability? Did it seem odd to him that a doctor would go to pieces the way she was doing? He'd been there, working on the resuscitation, too, yet he was the picture of tranquility, the antithesis of what she was. But he worked with patients, practiced medicine in its purest form, while she performed administrative duties and hadn't seen a patient, other than in passing on a stroll down one of her hospital's halls, since she'd left her residency.

Such a vast difference in the same profession. Part of her longing, and her need of late to rediscover her medical roots.

Suddenly, redeeming herself in this man's eyes seemed important. She didn't want him thinking of her as a total washout, even though that's how she felt. "I, um…I don't practice medicine," she said. "I guess that's why this hit me so hard. I don't do patient care at all. Just administrative work."

"Well, I do practice patient care, and death always hits me the same way. Especially when it's so senseless. There's nothing to be embarrassed about here, Doctor. And nothing to explain. I think the doctors who *don't* feel anything are the ones who should explain."

She gave him a weak smile. "Maybe I *should* go lie down for a little while, just to compose myself." The truth was, her initial reaction was to run away and hide, but now that she'd felt a little of his compassion seep into her, she didn't want to walk away from it yet. "After I sign the death certificate."

"I was there, too. If you'd prefer, I can sign it."

Susan nodded. "Thank you," she said. "And I'm sorry about being so…"

He held up his hand to stop her apologizing. "Nothing to be sorry about. You did a good job out there, Susan. Fought hard to save him. You have a right to whatever it is you're feeling."

Maybe she had the right to what she was feeling, but that didn't make her feel any better about it. She appreciated his support though. More than anybody could know.

The room Grant offered her was small and basic. One bed, one television, one telephone and little else. But it was clean, and the bed, as Susan gave in to the urge to lie down, was comfortable enough.

"Need anything?" Grant asked from the doorway. He seemed a little hesitant to enter.

"Maybe prochlorperazine. My stomach's a little upset."

"I'll have it sent right up," he said, still lingering there, not making a move one way or another. She watched him with a mixture of mild interest and wariness, waiting for him to leave, yet glad he didn't. He simply stood there...stood long enough for her to finally have a good look at him. Definitely tall— much more so than she'd thought at first, when she'd all but collapsed in his arms. Broad shoulders. Gorgeous bronze skin, black hair. He wore khaki shorts that hung to his knees and a loose-fitting flowered shirt, typical of what just about all the native islanders wore—and as far as she could tell he was a native islander.

"I know you're a doctor, but what kind? Family practitioner? A local, from the area here?" Strained, inept question, but she wanted to make conversation with this man. She wasn't sure why, though. Could it have had something to do with his good looks, and the fact that she didn't often have time to make idle chat with the opposite sex any more, and there was something about him that made her want to? Or just to keep him there just a bit longer?

He nodded. "Yep, a *very* local family doctor, born and raised right here. General family medicine is about all the clinic is set up to handle, unless it's an emergency, then we have a small emergency department. Nothing fancy there, though. We send the big cases to Honolulu."

"So, do you own the clinic?"

"No. I just run it."

"But you have a full-time staff? Other doctors, nurses…?" she asked, stopping short of requesting a full profile from him. My, wasn't she just the queen of useless chatter today?

"I'm the only full-time doctor but, yes, we're full service here, and we do have others coming and going. All the usual staff needed to run a forty-bed clinic," he said, looking mildly amused.

The next questions on the tip of her tongue were about the size of his average patient load, then about the profitability margins here. But she succeeded in stopping herself before she got them out, remembering this was not an interview to ascertain medical feasibility in the likelihood of a buyout. She was a temporary patient here, and he was her temporary doctor. It wasn't at all about business but, it seemed, that's all she was about. Even now. "Look, I'm sure you have other patients to see. I don't want to keep you, so if you could have someone bring me the prochlorperazine, I'll be out of your way within the hour."

He smiled, showing off perfect white teeth. "It could make you groggy. Too groggy to travel."

"Or it might not." He was trying to be nice and she appreciated that. "And I don't want to be taking up bed space here any longer than is necessary." She was thinking in terms of dollars and cents again, the corporate side of her ticking away so fast she couldn't control it. Which got to the heart of the problem she had to figure out. Did she really want to be all about corporate business? Or was there more out there for her? "It's not efficient, especially when I'm not really ill. You might have other patients…"

"If that becomes the case, I'll kick you out. But until then, how about you just relax? I'm getting the sense that it's something you don't do very often."

He didn't know the half of it. She *never* relaxed, and it appeared she didn't even know how. "How about I'll promise to try, and we'll leave it at that?"

"How about you put your head on the pillow and close your eyes?"

"And when I do I'll see that boy on the beach."

He finally entered the room in a casual swagger, propped himself on the wide windowsill, then twisted to face her. "For what it's worth, according to his buddy, Ryan Harris had been out drinking all night with his friends. He was hungover this morning, maybe he was even still a little intoxicated. His friends admitted that. On top of that, I seriously doubt he was all that experienced on the surfboard to begin with, seeing that he was a *haole*." Meaning foreigner. "From Chicago. No surfing there. Then when the big wave hit…" Grant swallowed hard, and a look of deep pain flashed across his face for a second, then disappeared. "It happens. A *malihini*…tourist…comes here for a short holiday, gets the idea that all he needs is a board and a good wave and he's a surfer." A sad sigh crept from his lips. "People think they know what they're doing, or overestimate their abilities, and they get careless. Add something else to the mix, like Ryan's condition, and it turns into a tragedy that probably could be prevented in most cases, if people acted smarter. But there's something about coming to Hawaii and losing inhibitions…"

"You deal with fatalities all the time?" The darker side of paradise, she supposed. The anguish it caused him was obvious. Dr Grant Makela was a man who cared deeply.

"Not all the time, but it happens often enough. We're the only medical clinic on this part of the island. There's no other help for miles, and I'm the only doctor who actually lives here, which makes me the one who gets called in most of the time. To the beach, to the hotels…" He shrugged, but it wasn't a shrug of indifference. More of acceptance. "There's more good than bad, though. Most of my encounters have a much better outcome than what you experienced. Like meeting you. That's definitely good."

To avoid his engaging smile and sensual mouth, she focused her gaze on his cheek.

Then she noticed dimples, and her quick glance froze in place. The man had honest-to-goodness dimples! And the most gorgeous onyx eyes. Grant Makela was a handsome man. Beyond handsome. Breathtaking, rugged, charismatic good looks. Natural charm. Natural ease. Not even one tiny speck of self-consciousness, she thought as she moved her stare down to his half-bare legs—nicely muscled, well bronzed like the rest of him. Her appraisal came to a stop at his sandals. Exposed toes. For some strange reason, that almost made her giggle. She'd *never* seen a doctor on duty with exposed toes. "I appreciate your understanding," she said. "I'm really just here as a tourist, not a doctor." Her shells. Her mornings on the beach. Three glorious days of paradise and now it was all over. She couldn't go back there.

Maybe it was time to call her father, apologize for leaving, and go back to doing what she was good at. *Which wasn't saving lives.* Dr Susan Ridgeway Cantwell was nothing if not pragmatic. She knew where her true value existed, and it wasn't languishing in a bed in an island clinic, talking on and on about nothing to the most positively gorgeous man she'd ever seen in her life.

Susan glanced down at Grant's toes again, of all things, and a rush of giddiness overtook her. Fatigue from emotional letdown, most likely. "Are you on duty right now?" she asked. One of her doctors would be reprimanded, or even dismissed, for dressing that way. For exposing toes.

"Twenty-four seven, at your service," he said, pushing himself off the window-ledge and sweeping into a courtly bow. "Like I said, we have a number of part-timers coming and going, but I'm the one and only full-time doc here."

"And they allow you to work dressed the way you are?"

He bent to look down himself, as if he hadn't been aware of the way he was dressed. Then he shrugged. "Island casual. That's the way we are around here. Patients are comfortable with it. Much more so than they would be with something more traditional—dress slacks, white shirt, tie, white lab coat." He faked a cringe. "What's good for my patients is good for me, too, actually."

She was good with it, too. At least, here on the island. She wouldn't have minded staying around for a while so she could watch a little more of Dr Makela's island-casual medicine, but she couldn't. Perhaps, in a way, that resuscitation attempt had answered some of her questions and made her decision for her. Where and how she worked now, making practical business decisions and never being called on to do CPR…maybe that's where she belonged. Maybe all her crazy feelings lately, about wanting to leave her admin duties and try patient care, were just that. Crazy.

"Look, I appreciate your helping me. What happened out there on the beach… Like I told you, I haven't been involved in patient care in a very long time and it got to me. I shouldn't have involved myself and maybe if I hadn't, someone else… *you*…could have had a better outcome. But I want to thank you for helping me, and if you send your bill, I'll sign it and write down all my contact information. Bill me there, and I'll see to it that you're paid immediately."

"No payment necessary," he said. "We haven't really done anything for you except give you a bed and a pill that will be here shortly, and that's not worth very much."

No payment? What kind of an odd clinic was this, that they didn't require payment for their services? "I don't expect charity, Doctor. I may not practice medicine but I'm fully able to pay for my medical care."

"We don't call it charity," he said. "We call it medical service with no strings attached."

"You've got to have strings attached," she argued. Strings, translated to mean money. She wasn't opposed to charity at all, and her facilities did make arrangements for those situations. But medicine was for profit. It had to be, to operate it on the large scale on which Ridgeway Medical operated—just closing in on one hundred medical properties in total. In fact, their Hawaiian acquisition would send them over the one-hundred marker. "How else can you operate if you don't expect your patients to pay?"

"We do have some private funding sources, many patients do pay, some have insurance. Basically, our needs are simple here, and people are as generous as they can be. But sometimes it's not money that constitutes generosity. And we accept that, too…generosity in other forms." He ran his fingers through his hair. "Treatment for a minor sinus infection paid for with a good haircut if that's all the patient can afford. Not what you're used to as a medical administrator, I'm sure, but I happened to need a haircut that day so it worked out."

"You do know you're every medical corporation's nightmare, don't you?" she said as she slid back into bed, finally putting her head down on the pillow. That spoken like the true corporate head she was. Bottom line, profit margin—the terms of her medical world on any given day, with the need of a good haircut not ever taken into account. They needed money in order to run all their medical facilities, to pay wages, to dispense medicine and perform surgeries, to make people better. A good haircut didn't get any of that done, but she did admire the senti-ment. Just couldn't relate to it. Or incorporate it into her clinics and hospitals.

"A medical corporation's nightmare maybe," he contended, "but every patient's friend. That's the part I like. It's the way medicine should be practiced, and it isn't done much that way any more."

Interesting man. Handsome like she'd never imagined in a man, and with ideals, too. She liked that. Liked it a lot.

She liked him, too. "But is it the part your clinic's *owner* likes?"

"I'm not sure what she likes," Grant admitted. "Especially lately. Look, why don't I go see about those pills? You need to rest, and I need to go see a patient. I'll catch up with you later, after you've had a nap." He chuckled. "And if you're a betting woman, maybe we could make a little wager on whether or not the prochlorperazine will make you groggy."

"Normally, I might take you up on that, but I'm afraid you'll win, and I'm not a very good loser." Thirty minutes later, after taking her pill, Susan shut her eyes and conjured up the image of her surfer Adonis while she drifted off to sleep. But just on that edge between full awareness and dream his image changed, then she was rocked gently into her bliss with the image of Dr Grant Makela fluttering around her fading consciousness.

# CHAPTER THREE

IT HAD been an awfully long day, and not a particularly good one at that, all things considered. Death had a way of flattening out the rest of the day, no matter how many good things came after it. The death of that Harris boy had been no exception even though, technically, he hadn't been the physician to work on him. Still felt the same, though. Still filled him with that down-to-the-bone tiredness that took a long, slow toll.

Dragging himself through the door of his home, a tiny cottage sitting directly adjacent to the clinic, Grant kicked off his sandals and dropped down into his bed. "Call me in an hour," he'd told the floor nurse as he'd left, even though he doubted he'd actually fall asleep. Not with images of that boy's death so fresh. Not with images of Dr Susan Cantwell's pain so vivid.

But not sleeping was okay, because he was doing it outside the clinic walls, which was what he needed from time to time…to get away. Even if only a few feet away. In his life, there weren't very many separations. Work, personal life, personal life, work…it was all pretty much the same. All of it relative to the fact that he kept his needs simple. Give him a good wave to catch once or twice a day, a great board for riding those waves, a few weeks a year to spend working with Operation Smiling Faces—a volunteer group of medics who did facial reconstruction for children living in areas where those services weren't available—let him have an occasional plane to fly, and his medical practice. That's all it took to make him happy.

A year ago, he'd thought Alana was part of that mix, but he'd been wrong about that. *Damn, had he been wrong!* So wrong, in fact, that he'd sworn off the finer sex for the foreseeable future. She'd had a beautiful face, nice curves, big goals. But none of those goals were his. On top of that, she'd had more needs than any one person had a right to.

A year of that and he was glad to be alone again. Still feeling the sting in a bad way, though.

Fluffing the pillow behind his head, trying to forget about Alana, Grant pushed his ex out of his head with thoughts of Susan Cantwell. *Kekoa*. Brave, courageous. That would be her Hawaiian name because she was brave and courageous, even if she wasn't feeling like it right now.

Susan… He'd enjoyed watching her on the beach these past few mornings. Certainly, he'd never expected that she was a doctor. A good one, judging by the way she'd worked so hard to save that boy when the inevitable had been obvious. That was dedication above and beyond the call of duty. And showed a refreshing passion.

Of course, he'd had his fair share of death to deal with here on the island, which had shaken him to the core each and every time. Some were catastrophic, some natural, but none ever nice. So he knew how she was feeling—knew that emptiness, that sense of loss, the feeling that you weren't good enough.

Yet the way she'd gone at the CPR—with such a vengeance. Definitely *kekoa*. Too bad she wouldn't be here long enough for him to help her understand that. But she was impatient. Someone who lived a complicated life. He could see, right off, that her mind was clicking away on a faster track than she showed on the outside. It was apparent in her eyes, in the way she'd looked at him, yet, at the same time, had looked far past him to something else that pulled in her deepest attention.

Once she felt steady enough, she'd be gone. Back to whatever kind of stressful life she lived. People like that came here all the time—came to relax, to get away from their tensions and look for something slower. They spent fifty weeks a year in a nerve-fraying lifestyle then figured that two laid-back Hawaiian weeks would cure everything. That was something he saw here every day, saw those people stretching out on the beach with their cell phone in one hand, popping antacids with the other, thinking that was unwinding. They got away from their life, yet they didn't.

Yes, that was Susan, or his first impression of her, anyway. And he usually trusted his first impressions. After all, he'd watched her wrestle with that damned floppy hat for three days now, always fighting the urge to do something more than merely take the holiday she'd planned for herself. It had been obvious, even from afar, that she wasn't the type to spend leisure time on the beach. She ached for more, lived and breathed a frenzied life. And now that he was up close…well, if he were a betting man, she'd be a sure thing. But his preference was the ones who fooled him, the ones who put that cell phone away and tossed their antacids into the trash. They were the long shots, but he'd take a long shot for the best results any day.

Unfortunately, he didn't see Susan as a long shot. Too bad because she needed to loosen up more than anybody he'd seen in quite a while. She wouldn't return to the beach, wouldn't wrestle with that hideous hat any more. And unless he missed his guess, she was already thinking about going right back to whatever she'd been trying to get away from.

Already, he missed that part of his morning where she

watched him from afar as he watched her. Well, that was a stupid thing to do, anyway, so maybe it was for the best that it was over. Getting attached to Susan *on any level* was a mistake. Getting attached to any woman was a mistake. Just look what the last woman in his life had cost him!

Stupid or not, though, Grant drifted off to sleep wondering what it would be like to work with Susan, to have her stay there at Kahawaii for a few days.

She felt rested this morning, which was hard to believe, having spent the night in the rather small hospital bed. She struggled to keep her eyes shut against the light streaming in through the window. She didn't want to look yet. Didn't want to wake up, or see the activities of all the early beach-goers off in the distance, swimming, relaxing, collecting shells…

Surfing.

There was no amount of rest sufficient for that, so she just wouldn't look. Out of sight, out of mind. Amazingly, as Susan indulged herself in avoidance for the next few moments, keeping her eyes shut to the world, the face of the young man on the beach she feared would pop into her mind didn't. Neither did the face of her surfer Adonis, even though she'd never seen his face…only fantasized it. But Grant Makela's face was there, as plain as if he were standing over her.

Grant Makela? Now, that shocked her. Why him?

*Because he was kind to me,* she reasoned almost immediately. Because he was her doctor, and people got attached to their doctors. Because he was the first person she'd really gotten to know, if only a little, here in Hawaii. She had her list of reasons, as anything else imitated interest, and if there was one thing Susan was not, it was truly interested in a man. From a distance, fine, but not up close, and absolutely not personal.

Once was enough, a lesson she'd learnt sufficiently with that brief and, oh, so boring marriage.

At the time she'd gotten involved it had seemed like the right thing to do. She had been approaching thirty, the clutch of not being married and a ticking biological clock getting to her, so she'd said *I do* to a nice man in a not too well thought-out decision. He was reasonably handsome, very successful with a fair amount of wealth in his own right. But bland... Good lord, the man's personality was like lumpy oatmeal, and the lumps were the only interesting part.

So she'd ho-hummed herself through six *long* months of bland with Ronald Cantwell before they'd come to a mutual understanding that they didn't work for each other. It had been one of those things that had seemed like a good idea at the time because there had been nothing at all offensive about him, although nothing about him had totally bowled her over either. Which, in retrospect, had been her first mistake, not being head over heels in love with the man with whom she'd intended spending the rest of her life.

One of life's little foibles was what she called it now. She and Ronald had gone their separate ways on reasonably good terms for a divorcing couple, and as a souvenir of her brief folly, she kept a name that wasn't her father's. That was actually a brilliant idea, keeping the Cantwell name, as working under her father's name did have certain disadvantages as in everyone's assumption, *like father like daughter.* Susan definitely *wasn't* like her father. Not in any aspect. So she'd hung on to her married name, promising herself that next time she married... Actually, there would be no next time, so the promise to choose herself a man who made her pulse race and her nerves tingle didn't mean anything. She wanted goose bumps, too. But there would be no man, so no racing pulse, no tingling.

And no goose bumps. That had such a sorry feeling to it.

Stretching, and finally giving in to the sunlight tempting her to take a look outside, Susan opened her eyes and glanced out the window, studying the people out there hurrying around. All of them had a sense of purpose, the way they were coming and going, it seemed. Or maybe that's just what she wanted to see since her own sense of purpose felt like it was slipping these days. "What to do with my life…" she whispered, turning away from the window.

Ridgeway Medical was her father's corporation, handed down to him by his father, and he'd spent years raising her up to take control of it. *This is all for you, Susan,* he'd always said. It had been just the two of them most of her life—her mother had died when Susan had been but a toddler—and her life had become, by default, an extension of her father's. She shared his interests, lived his life. Stood right behind him to do his job, and had been glad to do it.

But since her divorce she'd been…restless. Discontented. No particular reason why, especially given the life and all the opportunities she had. Hence the reason for her holiday. To get the old feeling back. To re-dedicate herself to what she did best. Except she was enjoying languishing here in bed—something she never did in her other life. And she liked sleeping late. Again, that was something that never happened in her real life.

Damn, she hated the mushy thoughts. They'd been creeping in so much lately, breaking up the normal way she thought. Usually, she was such a decisive person, yet recently…

*"Aloha kakahiaka!"* a cheery voice called from the doorway, breaking up the gloom already coming over her. "Good morning. My name is Laka."

Susan smiled at the bright-faced young woman coming through the door. Hawaiian obviously, with long flowing black hair and a smile that nearly lit up the room, the woman glided over to the bed with the smooth flow of an ocean wave, and stopped short of it. "Doc Etana thought you might like some breakfast before you leave this morning, so I'm here to take your order."

"My breakfast order?" Like in room service? As nice as Ridgeway hospitals and clinics were, they didn't offer room service.

Laka nodded. "We can fix almost anything you'd like, but my suggestion would be *pa'i palaoa hala kahiki.*"

They didn't bill you for services here, and they catered your breakfast? She was growing to like this place more and more with each passing minute. *"Pa'i pala..."* She shook her head, shrugging. "I can't pronounce it, but if that's what you'd rec-ommend, that's what I'll have," she said cheerfully, amazed by how such a simple thing was brightening her morning.

"It's a pineapple cake," Laka explained. "A recipe from Doc Etana's mother."

"Who's Doc Etana?" Susan asked. "I've heard that name mentioned before but I haven't met him."

Laka looked surprised. "He's Dr Makela. His first name is Etana, and that's what most of us call him."

One name for the natives, one for the outsiders? Briefly, Susan wondered if Grant, or Etana, kept his lives separated that way, much the way she did. She was Susan Ridgeway, yet she was Susan Cantwell. "Is he around this morning?" she asked, trying to sound nonchalant, even though she was anxious to see him.

"He's never around this early. He has his morning routines, but he'll be here soon enough. If you'd like to see another doctor, Dr Anai is here from Honolulu today. Should I call him for you?"

Susan shook her head. "No, that won't be necessary." It was

a bit of a disappointment. She'd wanted to see Grant Makela before she left, to thank him and to…well, she didn't know what else. It looked like that wasn't to be the case, though. Maybe that was a good thing, because there was no medical need to see him. She simply wanted to, no reason. In a life like hers, there wasn't room for any of that, so it didn't matter, even though she felt a little let down.

"Would you like to have breakfast on the *lanai?*" Laka asked. "Lovely view of the water from there. And the gardens, too."

The water. Another of her fantasies—her surfer Adonis. It was time for his morning visit to the beach, and she was missing it, which was a sure sign that matters were getting too far out of control with her. Come to paradise and forget all inhibitions, apparently. At least, that's what she was doing. It was also what she was going to put a stop to this very instant. "The *lanai* sounds very nice," she said, trying to mount resistance to fend off all these whimsies and wishes assaulting her. They were just another symptom of being overtired. The real reason she needed this holiday.

"Your clothes are in the closet," Laka said on her way out the door.

Her clothes—a swimsuit, and a baggy shirt to cover it. That didn't fit the occasion, but neither did the typical faded blue hospital gown she was wearing at the moment. "You wouldn't happen to have a pair of surgical scrubs handy, would you?" she asked before the nurse got away.

"We do, but no one around here ever uses them."

As Susan had noticed. Even the nurses wore Hawaiian-print dresses. "Well, if you could dust me off a pair…"

Ten minutes later, Susan seated herself on a white-painted bamboo chair at a white-painted bamboo table, glad to be outside in the fresh air again. Relaxing like this and getting outside was something she had no time for at home. Her communing with nature usually consisted of a minute or two on the way from the car to the building or the building to the car. So now any time spent with Mother Nature was a treat.

"Wonderful," she said to Laka, after taking a sip of passion fruit juice and finally allowing herself to relax.

"We specialize in wonderful here," Grant said from behind her, as Laka walked away.

A huge tingle crept up Susan's spine as a slight smile crept to her lips. "What's disappointing is that I may have to leave here, cut short my holiday and return to work," she replied, trying to be cautious about her galloping shivers lest she did something else to draw his attention to the goose bumps rising on her arms.

"On the mainland?" Grant stepped out from behind the hibiscus and stopped directly in front of the table. He looked fresh from the shower…wet hair glistening in the sun, shirt open a few buttons down and a bare chest with a few lingering droplets of water. She caught herself staring openly, and shifted her gaze to her glass of juice, grabbing it in both her hands just to steady herself.

"Actually, I'll be in Honolulu for a few weeks. On business. And I may get straight to that and skip the last of my holiday. There doesn't seem to be much point in it now." That much was true. There didn't seem to be reason any more. Her heart for it was gone.

"You mentioned you were an administrator—is that for a clinic or medical practice?"

She shook her head. "I…um…I work for a company in Dallas that buys struggling medical facilities and brings them back up to standard. I oversee medical operations, but more from an administrative perspective."

"That wouldn't be Ridgeway Medical, would it?" he snapped, his friendly expression turning into dark thunder.

She looked up at him, saw the deep frown on his face signal the change in his mood. "You've heard of us?"

"Heard of you? I've done nothing but hate you for the past six weeks. You've made my life pure hell ever since I knew that you existed." His words were angry, yet his voice was controlled and quiet.

That took her aback. Kahawaii Clinic wasn't on her current acquisitions list. She was sure of that. So what was this about? "Why? What have we ever done to you?" she asked, trying to tamp down the surge in her own temper. No need to fight him when she didn't know what it was about.

"Other than buying the clinic—what I hoped would be my clinic—and changing everything we're about?"

"But we're not! Yes, we're in the process of a nice deal on Oahu, but I know what properties we're looking at and this isn't one of them." It would be an ideal place for one of their clinics, she had to admit, but the Kahawaii name wasn't on the list.

"The hell it isn't! Mrs Kahawaii is in negotiations now, and she's indicated to me that she intends on signing the deal within the next couple of weeks, if I can't come up with a way to make a deal of my own. And she's signing with Ridgeway Medical."

"Kahawaii Clinic?" she asked, clearly perplexed.

"Officially, it's Hawaii North Shore Clinic, which we renamed it unofficially after its founder when he died."

That was a name she recognized. Susan sucked in an acute breath and immediately went on the defensive. "What's wrong with Ridgeway Medical?" she asked. "We upgrade medical care in areas where it's inadequate, and it's good medical care. We have excellent standards. We keep hospital doors open that would otherwise close, depriving a community of medical care, and we equip small clinics like this with the best medical technology money can buy. What's wrong with that?"

"You run roughshod over small clinics like this, forcing on them a standard that doesn't fit. You don't take into consideration the individual communities, and the people living there…what they need, what they want, what they'll accept. Your emergency doctors won't accept a haircut from a patient who can't pay in money but who has too much pride to take charity, and I doubt that any of your patients love their clinic so much that they'll volunteer to paint its exterior just as a matter of pride in the facility, like the people here did last year. You run institutional medicine, we run personal medicine. That's what's wrong with Ridgeway."

She really didn't have a defense for his argument because he was correct. But what he didn't understand was that they operated the way they did because it was the best for the majority of their patients. This was the argument she'd heard so many times, when various hospital and clinic administrators had found out their facility was being sold. People often resisted the change, didn't embrace it in any fashion. They fought against it, even though, like Grant, the decision wasn't theirs to make. And she truly hated the arguments, because lives were disrupted by what she and her father did. In the long run, it was for the best. But in the short term, just getting to that point, it was difficult, and that was the part of this business she hated the most. She detested being disruptive, hated putting the fear of change into people like Grant, who devoted their lives to an ideal, only to have that ideal ripped away from them. "Have you been to one of our facilities? Because if you haven't, I'd like to invite you—"

"Invite me to your indoctrination?" he interrupted. "Show me the proper corporate facility and tell me all this can be mine if I just adjust my attitude?"

Actually, that was correct. But she wasn't going to admit that to Grant, because that would just fuel his fire, and he had such a big fire going already that adding to it would prove nothing. The truth was, she felt bad about this. Always did, when it became personal. This time more than usual, though, because she liked this clinic, and she did see merit in it existing as it did, without change. With Ridgeway, though, change was inevitable, which made her sad for the little Kahawaii Clinic because, if she could be honest with herself, she'd pictured herself working in a setting like this. Part of that discontent she'd been feeling for a while had been that she wanted to connect to medicine in a way she wasn't allowed in her current capacity, and here, that connection would have been so easy.

But Grant was right. Kahawaii would change. She glanced down at his feet. He would have to wear regular shoes. No more bare toes. "Look, Grant, I know this isn't going to be easy for you. But we…Ridgeway Medical…does have its place. Small private hospitals and clinics struggle against the larger ones for a lot of reasons, and unfortunately most of those reasons are purely business. They can provide outstanding care, have an exemplary medical staff, sterling reputation, everything you want in a medical facility, but if they can't afford the latest MRI machine, for example, the patients who need an MRI for whatever reason go somewhere else, and it doesn't take too much of that to affect the bottom line financially. Patients who go away rarely ever come back. They find it more convenient to bundle up all their medical needs together and keep them at the one facility that can meet all their requirements. So when the bottom line takes hit after hit like that, with people leaving to find more services, the facility suffers. That's precisely why Ridgeway Medical is so important. We can keep that patient at that smaller facility and offer them everything they need there. In Indiana, for example, we own three small hospitals. Each, in itself, can't afford an MRI scanner, and the patient load is such that it's not warranted at any one of these facilities. All three were suffering when we stepped in, and the very first thing we did was buy a mobile MRI. It goes from facility to facility, and serves all three on a rotating basis. We're not losing our patients who need an MRI, and they're allowed to stay with the medical facility of their *first* choice because we pooled resources.

"I mean, people want to look at their medical treatment as something cozy and personal, but there's a huge, demanding business behind it that makes it work, and what we do is try to find a way to allow people to have the kind of medicine they want yet make the business aspects work to keep it that way."

"Is that in the company brochure?" he snapped. "Because if it's not, it sure should be. You've got the corporate verbiage down perfectly. It's a very good selling job if somebody wants to be sold, which I don't!"

In the official presentation they made, this was the part where they usually went to a multimedia presentation—graphs, charts, movie, testimonials. Which made Grant correct. She did have the company verbiage down…another of the reasons she wasn't so sure of her future in the company, as she was tired of the impersonal feel of it all. "Look, I don't know what I could say to make it right for you. Most people don't like the transition, and I understand that—"

"Do you, Susan? Do you really understand, or is that more jargon? Have you ever had everything you've come to count on transitioned right out from under you? And in the case of Kahawaii, have you even considered that you're transitioning it right out from under its patients, too? Look out there." He pointed to the gardens just off the end of the *lanai,* where Laka was helping an elderly woman take a walk down the path. The woman shuffled along on a walker, doing fairly well, actually, and Laka walked along with her, keeping a steadying hand on the woman's back. "Her name is Pearl. Replaced hip. Aged eighty-nine. How would *she* fare in one of your clinics?"

"We have rehab facilities—"

"She lives at home, Susan. Not in a rehab facility. Laka, or one of the other clinic workers, goes over there twice a day to help Pearl walk. She's living at home, where she's happy and comfortable. We send meals over from the clinic, too. All Pearl needs is a little assistance, and I can promise you that if we were to send her to a rehab facility, she'd give up and die. For her, staying at home means everything so that's what we're helping her do, and she's allowed her life and her dignity. It works out for us, too, as when we have children in the pediatric wards, she comes over to read stories to them. Or if we have babies staying here, she spends time sitting and rocking them, and singing to them when their parents can't be here. It's a valuable relationship, Susan, and I'm betting you don't have anything that personal in any of the Ridgeway facilities, do you?"

His voice was softening now, going from anger to…well, it could have been pride because there was a lot here to be proud about. But maybe it was love. Grant did love this clinic, and he had a passion for the way medicine was practiced here. Watching Pearl make her way along the path for a moment, Susan finally shifted her gaze back to Grant. "No, we don't, and I'm sorry. It would be nice to think that we could do something like that, but the truth is, when you have a hundred facilities to look after, it just can't be that way."

"Meaning the individual patient doesn't matter."

"Oh, the individual patient always matters, which is why we operate the way we do. We strive to give the best care to everybody who comes through our doors, but it's just not so…"

"Personal," Grant supplied.

"It's nice to have an ideal, Grant," Susan said, standing. It was time to leave. Truly, she did feel bad for what would of necessity happen at this little clinic, but it wasn't under her control. Somebody other than Grant was selling the place, and if she and her father didn't buy it, someone else would. Judging from the beautiful land on which it sat, that someone else might not be a company vested with medical interests. This would be the perfect place for a plush resort, or luxury condos… She wondered if Grant could see *that* handwriting on the wall, because it was written everywhere. Property this beautiful was scarce, and if Ridgeway didn't seal the deal…well, she didn't even want to think about the possibilities. "And I wish you well in yours. I'm sorry this won't be turning out the way you'd like it to, but I really don't make the deals. I just oversee the medical operations."

"You don't seem like the type," he said, as she stepped away from the table.

"And what type is that?" she asked, starting to bristle again.

"Corporate."

"And what is the corporate type supposed to seem like?"

"Not like you. Out there on the beach, when that boy drowned…the way you took it so hard…"

"I'm not unfeeling, Grant. I went to medical school just like you did, went through the same medical service rotations, learned the same procedures, dealt with the same kind of patients. And even though we don't agree on anything that Ridgeway Medical does, it's not fair to characterize me the way you're doing. Saying that I can't care, or that I don't have compassion because I'm corporate is the same as my saying that because you're only a country doctor you're too simple to understand the reasons a corporation like Ridgeway exists. I wouldn't do that because you do understand why we do what we do, even if you don't like it. And being a country doctor certainly doesn't make you backward, so I wouldn't ever say anything like that."

It was time to go, time to get back to the life she knew. She didn't have a fight with Grant, and didn't want to have one. He wouldn't believe that, but she did admire his passion for the kind of medicine he practiced. She even envied him that. It had been such a long time since she'd felt that kind of passion about anything, and she only hoped that once Ridgeway took over his clinic, he would hold on to it. Doctors like Grant Makela were rare.

Men like Grant Makela were even rarer.

# CHAPTER FOUR

"WORK here!" Grant shouted at Susan as she was about to climb into her rental car.

She spun around, assuming that he was chasing after her, but he wasn't. He was still standing on the *lanai.* Imposing figure of a man, she thought. That had been her first impression, and it hadn't changed. Standing there, in his shorts, Hawaiian floral-print shirt and sandals, he absolutely took her breath away. Forcing him to wear anything other than what he did was tantamount to a crime, but that was one of the changes on the horizon. "What?" she called back, not sure she'd heard him correctly.

"I said, work here. You said you were on holiday, so spend the rest of it working here."

He clearly wasn't going to come to her, so she walked halfway back to the *lanai,* then stopped. "And what would that prove?"

"You've never worked in one of your facilities, have you?"

Was that a devious little smile on his face? It was hard to tell, staring into the sun the way she was, but she would have sworn she saw a smile cross his lips. "I oversee corporate medical policy, but I leave the individual hospital and clinic admin matters to the hospital administrators."

"Not administration, Susan. That's not what I'm asking. I'll bet you've never donned a lab coat, hung a stethoscope around your neck and set off as a practicing doctor in *any* of your medical facilities. You know, treat strep throats, prescribe for bronchitis, that kind of thing? You haven't done it, have you?"

Such a devious smile, and he *was* challenging her, as it turned out. He probably thought he'd get her to work here for a few hours, for her to see what the *real* medical world was like, then change her mind. Except it didn't work that way. Too bad, too, because if she had it in her to give him his clinic, she probably would. "What I've done is make it possible for hundreds of doctors to treat thousands of patients with strep throats and bronchitis." She liked his gutsiness, though.

"Then work here, as a doctor. Let me rephrase that. Work here like a doctor who isn't encumbered by the dictates you put on the doctors working for Ridgeway Medical."

"How long?" she asked, surprised she had. She really had no intention of doing this, but she was the moth being drawn into the flame. The closer she got the more she knew she would surely meet an awful demise, yet something in her was wired to keep moving toward the flame. And she was a heck of a lot smarter than that moth. "If I were to stay here and work, which I'm not going to do, how long would you expect me to do this?"

"How many more days left of your holiday?"

He was serious. Grant was actually serious about this! "Six, including today."

"Then I'll take six, including today."

This was crazy. She was actually entertaining the invitation. "And what's in it for me, if I do this?" Not only entertaining it, showing enough interest in it that his devious smile was growing larger.

"Awareness of what it's like at the other end of the spectrum. You sit at a desk and make decisions for lives that never touch

yours. Here, you'll make decisions for lives that do touch yours
and that will make you a better administrator."

"You're hoping that I'll change my mind, aren't you? That
when I leave here in six days I'll wave some kind of a magic wand
and you'll miraculously have your clinic the way you want it."

"Yes. And I'll take my opportunities wherever I can get them."

It was an honest arrangement, but it occurred to Susan that
Grant didn't know she was one of the corporate officers. Not
just one of the officers, actually. One of the owners. For now,
perhaps it was better that he didn't. Especially as she was
tempted to take him up on his offer. Funny how it coincided
with her restlessness to get back to regular patient care.

Well, what would it hurt to give it six days then see what
happened? For that experience, she'd discover if her restlessness was a passing whim or a valid problem. Maybe she'd find
out she was truly cut out for admin work after all. Or maybe it
would show her, once and for all, that she *could* be a practicing doctor. Besides that, she'd be in a good position to make
recommendations to the Ridgeway board about Kahawaii, not
that anybody on the board would necessarily agree with her. So,
however it happened, this seemed like a good opportunity for
her. "No promises, because I don't know how these next days
will turn out. I may or may not make the recommendations you
want. And the board may not listen to me if I do recommend
what you want. If that's agreeable, with no strings attached to
the outcome, I'll give you my next six days." Those words surprised her almost as much as they surprised him, judging from
the look on his face. But why not? She did have the time, and
she could think of worse things to do than spend a few days
with Grant, in paradise no less, even though it was pretty clear
they weren't going to get along famously. How could they,
given that they were at odds?

"I'm in charge," he warned, like he had to. Of course he was in charge. She wouldn't have had it any other way, especially given her lack of regular doctoring these past years.

"You're in charge."

A tight little frown popped up between his eyes, like he was adding up a list of pitfalls in this arrangement he'd just proposed. First, she wasn't well practiced. Second, she wanted to quash the current Kahawaii operation. Third, she wanted to infuse Ridgeway practices. Yes, that was the list Susan imagined he was beginning to form, one that could have gone on and on from that, but she didn't want to think about it because, it seemed, she was about to be put to work. That's what was making her nervous now. Agreeing to be a practicing doctor was one thing, but actually doing it...

"The locals tell me you have another name," she said, deliberately changing the subject for a moment. She needed time to catch her breath, to think about what she'd just done. Maybe back out once the brunt of it hit her.

"You're backing out already," he accused.

"I'm trying to make polite conversation," she counted.

"In the middle of a disagreement?"

"Are we still disagreeing? I thought we'd settled all that for now."

He chuckled. "Nothing's settled, Susan. It's just being avoided temporarily."

"And in the spirit of avoidance, I was asking about your name. No ulterior motives here, Doctor. I was just curious." He walked across the *lanai,* then crossed over the parking lot, stopping just a few feet in front of her, where he studied her face for a moment, making her more nervous than ever as she knew exactly what was written there. If she'd had a mirror to look in, she'd have seen a virtual masterpiece of insecurity and self-doubt. The implications of this arrangement she'd just made were beginning to set in now, and the enormity of what she'd promised to do... Crazy! What was she thinking, agreeing to work as a practicing doctor?

"My native name—Etana. It means strong, or firm. It's what my mother called me, so most of the people here still use it."

"Which suits you," she said rather weakly, as her hands began to tremble.

He shrugged. "Grant's good, too. It was my grandfather's name. He was a missionary to the islands."

"A *haole?*" she asked.

"A foreigner, yes. For a time. But once he settled here he never left. People tend to do that here. Come for a little while and never leave." He smiled, but this time the deviousness of it was missing. It was a genuine smile, and a gentle one. "The lure of the islands."

"And you use his name now because...?"

"Let's just say that I wasn't the perfect child. Got into a lot of trouble. People here still remember that and associate it with Etana. So when I returned here after medical school I had the bright idea that changing my name made me a new person."

"Has it worked?" It hadn't for her, because Susan Ridgeway by any other name was still Walter Ridgeway's daughter.

He laughed, shaking his head. "Do you hear anybody calling me Grant?"

"Well, maybe in time..."

"Or not. Sometimes, you are who you are, and nothing will change that fact. Not even a different name. I treat Omar Lahani for angina, he takes my advice, takes the pills I prescribe, but he never forgets that I was the one who broke the brand-new picture window he'd just had put in his house."

"Playing ball?" she asked. "An accident?"

"With a rock. On purpose. I was nine, the plate glass looked so…breakable. Changing my name hasn't changed Omar's memory of what I did. I was hoping it would, but I was wrong."

Just like she was a Ridgeway no matter what she called herself. That was a fact that wouldn't be changed either. "So are you still the bad little boy? Or is that just a lingering perception?"

"Not in deed—at least, not any more. But I'm not so sure I really want to put it that far behind me, because some of that is what made me who I am. In my culture we have a strong belief that we each have a personal destiny to fulfill, and I think that everything I was became part of that destiny."

A destiny to fulfill. She did believe that, but she wasn't as sure that she'd found her personal destiny as Grant was that he'd found his own. She envied him that sureness in his life. "Are you absolutely positive that you want me working here?" she asked, changing the subject back to the situation between them. "I'm not…" She swallowed hard, trying to fight back the nervousness threatening to take over in her. "Grant, I know it seemed like a good idea in the heat of the debate, but now I'm not really sure I should do this. And no matter what you think of me and my corporate ways, I don't want to give bad patient care."

"A deal's a deal, Dr Cantwell. I'm not backing out, but whatever you choose to do is up to you."

Well, she never backed down from a challenge either. Swallowing hard again, she braced herself for what was to come next. "When do I start?" she asked, sounding a lot more brave about this than she was feeling.

"Immediately. I think duty in our little emergency room will work nicely. We treat pretty much every injury associated with the beach, as well as the usual. The basic kinds of things you went to medical school to learn. Complicated or serious cases are transferred to Honolulu if at all possible."

*You know why you're going to medical school, Susan, and it's not to become a practicing physician.* Her father's words were plaguing her now. *Anyone can do that, but not just anyone can take over Ridgeway Medical. You learn everything you need to know while you're in medical school and Ridgeway will be all yours one day.*

Everything she needed to know… How ironic that her subsequent years learning business admin had been more relevant to running a medical corporation than her medical training. In her opinion, though, the best medical administrators were doctors, and they did need the training in both worlds.

"You're good, Susan," Grant continued, "or I wouldn't be asking you to do this. Well, that, and the fact that having one more doctor here will give me more time to try and find a way to stop you from taking over the clinic."

That caught her attention. "Do you think you can?" she asked, purely because she was interested. Not interested because she was a Ridgeway. She genuinely wanted to know.

"Maybe I do," he said cautiously.

She actually laughed out loud. "And maybe you don't. I get it, Grant. You don't trust me." Which hurt, but she couldn't blame him. She was the proverbial wolf in sheep's clothing here, yet she did wish they were on better terms with each other. "Well, then," she said, not sure where to go with this. It was becoming awkward now, which meant the graceful way to end this little scene was to shake hands on the deal then back away. "It's a deal. I'll go to work…immediately." She extended her hand to him, the way she'd extended her hand to countless others in various business deals. "Just tell me what you want me to do."

A little spark caught between them. She felt it and liked the touch of him—the softness of his skin, the gentle way he held her hand. No one, not even Ronald Cantwell, her ex, had ever touched her like that, had ever made her crave the feel of another person's skin the way she was craving it from Grant right now. Which was why she put an abrupt stop to it. She liked it too much. In fact, she liked everything about Grant Makela too much, which could have been a problem, except Grant didn't seem the type to cavort with the enemy, and to him she was the sworn enemy. So didn't that make her crazy, staying here under these conditions? The answer to that was yes, but she wasn't ready to leave, and it had as much to do with her restlessness as it did with her feelings for Grant.

"One day," Grant said. "We'll take it one day at a time, and either one of us can withdraw from the deal at the end of the day. And what I want you to do for starters is go to the emergency room and take care of Mr Morimoto. He comes in twice a week and we check his feet and legs for signs of neuropathy. He doesn't see so well, and he has fragile veins, prone to blood clots, so we take a look, listen to his heart and lungs, that kind of thing."

"Twice a week?" she asked, more from interest than anything else.

"In my medical world, yes," Grant said defensively. "Which I'm sure differs from anything you would do, but we like preventative precautions here. In the long run, it's in the patient's best interest."

"Actually, you're right."

"That's all?" Grant asked, somewhat surprised. "No arguments?"

"Big medicine isn't a monster, Grant. It's a necessity. We do what we do because it's the best way to tend to a lot of patients. You can argue about that, and question our methods for the entire time I'm here, but we're really on the same side. If Mr Morimoto needs to be seen twice a week, then that's the medical care he should have. I wouldn't dispute that."

"But would Ridgeway Medical, *the corporation,* dispute it?"

She really did want to change his mind about Ridgeway, but she wasn't sure that was going to happen. Grant was like a tomcat with its back up, screaming at its sworn enemy, which in this case was Ridgeway Medical. Tomcats never made up to each other and, as disappointing as it seemed, she doubted Grant would ever make up to Ridgeway, which was going to make it awfully tough on him if Ridgeway succeeded in buying the clinic.

Suddenly, it occurred to Susan that if that deal went through, Grant might not stay. He might find the takeover, and the new rules, so intolerable that he would walk away from Kahawaii Clinic. That would be such a loss. "Look, I have a suggestion. For the sake of us working together here, could we agree that we disagree, and get on with it? I don't want to be at odds with you, Grant. And I don't want you being at odds with me. I'm sorry about the situation, but it's not in my hands, and it's not in yours, so how about we just make the best of it for the few days I'm here? Oh, and for what it's worth, I hope that you can work out something to buy this clinic before Ridgeway does. I think it belongs with you."

She meant that. There were certain things that *shouldn't* change, and this was one of them. But in the scheme of things, whether or not Ridgeway absorbed Kahawaii Clinic into its structure wasn't up to her. Ridgeway's board made those decisions, with strong recommendation from her father, who could overrule board suggestions if he had a mind to. Which he rarely did. Yet in her capacity she merely worked with the consequences of those decisions. It was her choice, as her father was more than eager to bump her into a better position.

"It's personal, Susan. I hope you understand that. What could happen to the clinic is very personal. I know you're just doing your job, but…" he shrugged "…so am I. Only my job is my life. My patients are my friends. It's all one and the same."

Well, it wasn't so different for her. Her job was her life, too. Like for Grant, all one and the same. Except in her life there weren't friends. Business associates and business acquaintances, but not real friends. It seemed like he might have the better situation here.

"Are we going to be okay enough to work together?"

He nodded. "I want you to see what it's like, practicing medicine in a place like this. I promise you, Susan, it's like nothing you've ever experienced." His voice softened, and the hard edge melted from his eyes. "And I don't have anything against you, really. In fact, I rather liked you until I found out you were with Ridgeway."

"You don't like me now?" That devious little smile crept back to his lips, and that little glint reappeared in his eyes. Susan almost sighed in relief.

"We'll see," Grant said, then walked away.

Well, it wasn't the best exchange she'd ever had but it wasn't the worst by far. Maybe, just maybe, the next six days weren't going to be so bad after all.

"Doc Etana said you are one good lady doctor," Mr Morimoto said, as he climbed up onto the exam table.

He was an older man, but Susan couldn't tell how old. He had flawless dark skin, salt-and-pepper hair and sharp black eyes. "Doc Etana is too kind," she replied, purposely averting her eyes until he was settled and his hospital gown was arranged neatly over his lap. Admittedly, she was nervous about this. He was her first real patient in years. "But I appreciate the compliment."

Mr Morimoto didn't respond. Rather, he folded his hands in his lap and watched her. So she set about her exam. Took his blood pressure, listened to his heart and lungs, looked in his eyes and ears, probed his belly. When she got around to his leg exam, bending to examine his feet, Mr Morimoto laid a hand on her shoulder. "You should talk more. You have a nice voice."

Susan looked up at him. "I'm not very good at small talk." In other words, she had no bedside manner…not good, not bad. Once, when she had been a resident, her supervisor had complimented her on having such a nice bedside manner…one of the nicest he'd ever seen. But that had been long ago, and in her medical reality bedside manner didn't matter. Which was why she was so out of practice. "Most of the time I don't deal directly with patients, so I haven't mastered the fine art of chit-chat. You know, how's the weather?"

"Fine. Balmy. We could use a little rain, though."

"What?" she asked.

"You asked about the weather, and I answered. That's small talk." He gave her a wide grin. "And how long has it been since you've examined a patient, might I ask?"

Running her hands first over his left foot, then his right, she frowned as she counted back the years. "I think it's been about five." Finding nothing wrong with his feet, she moved her exam up to his ankles and calves.

"And you like this medicine you practice where you don't deal with patients?"

"I should, as I've spent so many years doing it."

"An evasive answer, my dear. Which is very telling."

"Is it?"

He nodded, as her hands slid to the back of his right calf, then his left. "I was a teacher at the university here, retired last year. When anybody asked me if I liked what I did, I always said yes right away. Then if I had complaints, those came next. The truth always comes out at first, when you're not thinking so hard about it. I asked you if you like what you do and you answered that you should, which to me says that you don't."

"Career crisis," she said. "I've been wondering, lately, if I took the wrong career path at the start."

"It's never too late to change."

"But in my situation it's not too easy either." She examined his legs up to his knees, then continued on up to his thighs. "I'll figure it out, though."

"That's why you're here? To figure it out?"

"Something like that," she said, completing her check. "So, do you have any leg pain? Have you had any notable changes?"

"Everything's the same. Nothing has changed in three years, but you can't be too careful, can you? One little change can affect so many things."

That much was true. It could. And in her case, no matter what she did, it would. "Do you exercise?"

He nodded. "I walk. Swim. Bicycle three times a week. All things in moderation, and it works out."

"Well, everything seems fine to me."

"And wasn't it a much more enjoyable exam once you started talking? It puts your patient at ease and, in some cases, even puts the physician at ease."

"It showed that much?"

He laughed as he started to climb down from the exam table. "I'm afraid that it did. But you'll get better. Give yourself another week or two and you'll turn yourself into a regular conversationalist."

Another week or two... Mr Morimoto had no idea what was going to happen in another week or two. Of course, at this point, neither did she.

# CHAPTER FIVE

ROUTINE care. That's what he'd assigned Susan to do in their emergency department, such as it was—five cubicles, the basic equipment, adequate supplies. All she'd been doing for the past four hours now had been treating cuts, bruises, sunburn, stomachache, and various other routine complaints, the lot of the emergency department, he did have to admit. Nothing glamorous, nothing exciting, but what he'd noticed every time he'd looked in on her had been that she'd been smiling. Tentatively at first, bubbling now. She was moving from patient to patient with such ease, treating each minor case as if that person were the most important patient in the world. In only a few words, Dr Susan Cantwell became their friend and someone they trusted. For the locals, who were set in their ways and didn't always welcome outsiders—and that included the people who gave them medical care—what she was accomplishing with them was nothing short of a miracle. Tourists in medical trouble they hadn't anticipated found Susan's bedside manner a blessing during a trying time.

It was a gift. She had a natural flair for patient care and she was happy doing it—the kind of doctor everyone wanted to be, but the kind most never became. There was a glow on her face attesting to that, making him wonder why she'd stuck herself behind a desk like she had. For the money? Certainly, a woman with a position such as hers had to have a very handsome income. Yet he didn't see her as someone who cared much about that. But there had to be something drawing her to the admin position. So, was it a passion for providing the kind of care she claimed Ridgeway provided? Did she truly believe that what Ridgeway did was best for all their clinics and hospitals? That being the case, and he suspected it was, then no matter how nicely she responded to the patients, and no matter how she seemed to like what she was doing here, it wouldn't matter. She wouldn't change her mind, which meant he was sunk, unless Mrs Kahawaii had a change of heart about selling Kahawaii Clinic. He wasn't pinning many hopes on that, though.

A sorry mess overall, and on top of that he was attracted to Susan, which made it even sorrier. She wasn't quite the enemy, but close enough. Talk about falling for the wrong woman! Again! Well, he certainly had quite a proclivity for that, didn't he? Of all the people on this planet to catch his attention, his future boss? And one, at that, whose policies and procedures he already hated.

That was definitely a proclivity for the wrong woman! But knowing that and waging all the logical arguments with himself wasn't correcting a thing because he was still attracted.

Now, as he watched her tend to a rather nasty case of sunburn on a teenage girl, who paid more attention to the amount of skin she revealed than she did protecting it, he considered all the details of his turmoil—the impending sale of Kahawaii. Big hospitals gobbling up little ones. Like it or not, Kahawaii was affiliated with one of the larger hospitals in Honolulu. Had to be, to have a continual source of doctors and other medical services that couldn't be provided here otherwise. Yet that hospital was struggling to stay open for reasons he didn't know, and in its affiliation with Kahawaii came the problem because as that hospital went, so did the clinic.

In other words, his nice little village medical practice could give way to exactly what he and Susan had argued about, and he deserved a large share of the blame for that. "Damn you, Alana," he muttered, as he watched Susan glide across the room to see her next patient, Mrs Hamakolea. She was a feisty one. Old. One of the many who was set in her ways. Not particularly friendly to anyone and suspicious as hell of newcomers and outsiders. Even now she didn't totally believe *he* was a full-fledged doctor. In her mind he was still Etana, the young boy who stole pineapples from her garden. Which he had been, years ago. He was still apologizing for it after all this time. And now Susan was about to meet the lady's wrath. Mrs Hamakolea's scowl was in place. Five feet tall, half as round as she was tall, long, black hair pulled up into a tight knot on the top of her head, her arms crossed tightly over her chest, she was a force to be reckoned with.

For a moment Grant took pity on Susan, for what she was about to face, and considered stepping in to rescue her. She didn't deserve Mrs Hamakolea. But…what was that? Mrs Hamakolea was smiling? Actually smiling! And laughing. She was going along willingly with Susan to the exam cubicle, like they were long-lost friends, and being very pleasant about it. Of all the amazing things that could happen, he hadn't expected this.

Grant sighed as he went to his next patient—another surfing accident. Probably a cracked rib. The blunt anger over what Alana had done was slipping down over him again as he plodded along the hall, trying to shake off his sullen mood before he had to put on his doctor facade. She'd walked off with his life's savings. Money he'd saved to buy the clinic, which consequently would cause Mrs Hamakolea and so many others like her to suffer as she would never agree to something more structured in her medical treatment, the way Ridgeway would structure it. She and the others were comfortable and if Kahawaii was sold, and their ways forced on her, she wouldn't come in, as simple as that. With her high blood pressure, that could and probably would be dangerous.

*The significance of what Alana had done couldn't be measured in the dollars and cents she'd stolen from him.*

Dr Kahawaii had made Grant a generous offer to sell him the clinic. It had been the plan even before Grant had gone off to medical school. But then, after he'd come back home and established himself, he'd gone and invited Alana in to live with him. In retrospect, he realized it had been an attempt to make himself seem more *adult* in a community that still saw him as a little boy. Instant acceptance, a stupid folly, stupid move. He hadn't known her. Hadn't loved her. Hadn't paid enough attention to her either, which had ended up costing him everything he'd had, and the dollar-by-dollar repayment she was making now, arranged by her lawyer to keep her out of jail, wasn't enough for him to go through with the sale. He'd had to back out, pretty well cementing many opinions of him that he was still Mrs Makela's bad boy and medical school hadn't changed him.

Naturally, Dr Kahawaii had been disappointed by all that, and a little let down by Grant, because he'd never seen him as that bad boy. In turn, Grant truly hated letting down the one person in this world, other than his mother, who'd had so many great expectations of him. But the old man had gone ahead and made alternate arrangements that would allow Grant more time and give him smaller payments on that purchase. Before that agreement had been executed legally, however, Dr Kahawaii had dropped dead of a heart attack, and his widow hadn't been so keen on the long-term arrangements of the sale. She'd given

Grant six months to come up with a fitting down payment, which was generous of her, but six months weren't nearly enough for him to earn back what she required, given his current finances.

So now, at the six-month point, while nothing had been finalized, Mrs Kahawaii was entering into discussions over the disposition of the clinic. He didn't fault her for what she was doing, yet he wasn't about to give up on finding a way to keep the clinic until the deed was done. Miracles were known to happen, and maybe she would extend him six more months. What he could accomplish in that time he didn't know, but six months was six months and who knew what might happen along the way? The worst she could do was refuse him after all.

So, the day after next he had an appointment in Kane'ohe to go and see Mrs Kahawaii, to face the best, or worst, outcome. Until then he was still searching for options. And, yes, Susan was an option. In the best-case scenario, she would see the merit of leaving the clinic alone, and make that recommendation to her superiors.

It wasn't much to hang a hope on, but it was better than nothing.

In the meantime, he had to quit watching her, quit being distracted by all the good parts that didn't belong to Ridgeway Medical, because the little bit of trust he did still have left for the fairer sex was enough to get him into trouble. It was like stealing Mrs Hamakolea's pineapples. They were the biggest and the best, and he'd known it had been wrong. But, damn, those pineapples were tasty. Which was why he had gone back to her pineapple field on occasion. He simply hadn't been able to resist. Come to think of it, though, they had always got him into trouble. Trouble he was still paying for today, he decided as Mrs Hamakolea strolled out of the emergency cubicle with a wide grin on her face that turned into a dark scowl the instant she spotted him.

"Any problems?" he asked, following Susan into the nursing station. She was wearing scrubs, her blond hair was pulled back, her blue eyes were sparkling, she wore no makeup, and looked absolutely stunning. Grant blinked twice, trying to get that out of his mind. He would certainly do himself a service thinking of Susan as the enemy, but he just couldn't do it. "Especially with Mrs Hamakolea?" He gave the old lady a pleasant smile as she scowled her way right past him and all the way out the door.

"Nothing a second-year med student couldn't handle," Susan said, her voice actually quite bright. "Routine complaints, some minor beach injuries. And Mrs Hamakolea is lovely. A very sweet lady, in fact. She's invited me to her house to sample her pineapples. She said they're the best anywhere around here."

"You're going?"

"Later this afternoon, when I'm off duty. She promised to bake me a pineapple cake."

He chuckled, a tinge of admiration creeping in. Susan had scored big in a way she didn't even understand. "I'm betting she didn't invite me along. Did she?"

"No. Not that I recall. But she's so nice. I'm sure she wouldn't mind…"

Holding up his hand to stop her, he shook his head. "Mrs Hamakolea and I go way back. I had, shall we say, a *misspent* youth. Some of the people here still hold it against me, so trust me when I say that Mrs Hamakolea, in particular, doesn't want me coming to her house, especially when eating her pineapple is involved. So, how is your day going so far?"

"Not bad. Like I said, everything seems fairly routine."

"And you're enjoying it?"

"Would you care?"

That little defiant streak of hers was coming out again. He liked it, actually. It added extra spark to her eyes. Very sexy. "You tell me, Susan. Should I care?"

"Well, one of us has to, and as you don't think somebody like me could, then I suppose you have to care, don't you?"

"Well, then, because I have to care, let me ask again. Are you enjoying your little venture into island medicine…patient care, everyday complaints? You know, medicine on a personal level?"

"It's not in your eyes," she said.

"What?"

"All that pent-up contention you want to vent on me. You're trying to let it out, but it's just not there."

"And you're avoiding answering me. Which means only one thing…"

"What?"

"That you like what you've been doing here." It was a big leap to take, making that assumption, but he hoped he was right.

"I like practicing medicine," she did admit.

"But here. Do you like practicing it *here,* the way we do it?"

Susan glanced away from Grant as a young woman with a crying toddler walked up to the admittance desk. "It looks like I have another patient," she said, spinning away.

*You're saved for the moment,* he thought as he headed off to find a tube of ointment for his sunburn patient. *But you'll answer my question, Susan.* And for the first time since he'd proposed this crazy arrangement to have her here as a doctor, he was modestly optimistic that she would admit that she did like the way medicine was practiced at Kahawaii.

Or maybe that was wishful thinking. Maybe he was reading something into her that just wasn't there. But he certainly hoped not.

* * *

It was mid-afternoon, and the first rush of patients had died down to a trickle. In fact, as Grant appraised the emergency room, there was no one being treated, and no one even waiting. No one with appointments in the clinic either. "Are you busy right now?" he asked Susan, as he put away his last patient chart and handed the figurative reins over to Dr Anai, one of the part-time docs.

"Not unless something comes in. Since it's slow, I was thinking about taking a break." Her first of the day, and she was ready for it. Amazingly, her time had passed quickly. She'd enjoyed every minute of it, and was quite surprised to find that it was getting on in the day. She'd probably pay for all the physical exertion tomorrow, but for now she was charged, still had plenty of energy left. "I'd like to grab something to drink before I go back on duty." She placed her last chart in the rack next to the desk and started to walk back around to the hall, but stopped short of Grant. "Are you asking me to do something? Is that why you're here?"

"Take a walk with me. Actually, a house call."

"You make house calls?"

Surprise registered on her face. Of course it would, he thought. House calls weren't a practical consideration for anyone from Ridgeway. Too personal. "If that's what it takes. And this patient prefers to have a female along. She's old-fashioned, doesn't care to have a man treat her."

"Why do I get the feeling you're not telling me everything?"

"There's not much to tell." He held out a canvas bag.

"That's assuming I'm going with you." She took the bag, peeked inside, then shut it. "Canned meat? That's all that's in here."

"Different cures for different folks. You'd be surprised what a little canned meat will do."

"Well, now you've got me intrigued, so I suppose I'll have to go, won't I?"

"Jeep's outside the door."

"I thought we were going to take a walk."

He chuckled. "Believe me, we will. But we need to drive to where that walk starts." He really hadn't intended to ask her along to see Grandma Moana. But something about a two-hour trip with Susan seemed appealing enough for him to ask Laka, one of the Kahawaii nurses, to stay behind today. Normally, Laka went out alone on these calls to Moana, as there wasn't really any reason for one of the doctors to go simply to take a test to check the old woman's blood sugar. But after fretting about finding a solution to Kahawaii's problems for the past several hours, he needed the excuse to get away, to put some distance between himself and the clinic so he could clear his head and restore a little objectivity. Pressures were building up, and having Susan here was more of a reminder of those pressures than he'd expected. All that was causing him a real banger of a headache. Yet here he was, taking her along with him on his little retreat from reality. It didn't make sense, trying to find a cure for the headache by spending more time with the source of it. Not exactly sound medicine, was it?

Checking his supplies after he climbed into the Jeep, he counted out a month's worth of glipizide, a drug used to keep Moana's marginally high blood sugar in line, a month's prescription of lisinopril to keep her blood pressure down, and a bottle of antacid tablets. She liked the minty, over-the-counter variety.

"So, tell me all about this patient we're seeing," Susan said, as they started off down the road. She squirmed in her seat, and crossed her arms protectively over her chest, telling him this was definitely not a social outing.

"She's like everybody else here. She wants her medical care on her own terms."

"And her terms include prescription medicine and canned meat. How can that be a practical use of time? I mean, I don't begrudge the woman her pills, but wouldn't it be better to find a way to get her to come to the clinic than take the clinic personnel out of the clinic to accommodate her?"

"No," he said, quite bluntly.

"Why not?"

"She deserves to get what she wants. And she does pay for it."

"What? A pineapple, or another haircut?"

"She makes the uniforms we wear. All the floral prints…"

"Those you could probably buy quite inexpensively somewhere."

"I suppose we could, but then Grandma Moana wouldn't feel useful, the way she does now. She plays an important part in the clinic, and she knows it. So what would you have me do, take her sense of purpose away from her? Because that's what would happen if we changed this deal."

"Well, maybe in this one instance the way you've worked out the arrangement isn't so bad."

"Maybe?" He cocked an amused eyebrow. She just didn't want to give in, but he was sensing a small victory here. The persuasion of Dr Cantwell might not be so bad after all.

"Okay, it's nice. I'll admit it. She does lovely work and it does benefit the clinic. For the cost of a few inexpensive pills it doesn't seem so bad. But why the canned meat?"

She was so good at that…sliding right out of one subject she didn't want to talk about and into another that was more comfortable for her. But he would allow her that diversion. He'd had his little win, and for now he was happy with it. No need to taunt her or rub it in.

"Canned meat, specifically corned beef, is considered a delicacy. There are a lot of stories why, but the one I like best, my mother's version of the story, is that during the Second World War food was in short supply, other than the fruits grown here. Especially meat protein other than fish. So food was brought in by the US military to supplement the low supplies in the islands, and canned meat was one of the only sources of non-fish protein available in large quantities. People came to love it, and that love affair hasn't stopped. A nice can of corned beef is about as good as it gets for a lot of people here. They'd rather have that than just about anything else, but it's expensive as hell as it has to be shipped in from the mainland, so it's a treat, a delicacy that's not too affordable."

"And Grandma Moana loves her corned beef."

"Don't worry. It doesn't come out of clinic funds."

"I didn't ask that," she said defensively.

"But you wanted to. The question was already on your lips, wasn't it?"

"It's a practical question, and I'm a practical person. Maybe I was considering asking it."

Once again he cocked an amused eyebrow. "Maybe?"

"What do you want from me, Grant? I already admitted that the uniforms Grandma Moana makes are a good idea. Isn't that enough for you?"

"Once is never enough." He meant that, too. But he meant it in ways that had nothing to do with this conversation and had everything to do with things he could only have fantasies about with Susan.

He was enjoying this, enjoying spending time with Susan, talking to her. It was something he'd never really done with Alana. He hadn't had much time for her; they'd never talked. The whole relationship had been about convenience, and what he'd thought convenient had turned out to be anything but. Suddenly the whole Alana debacle came back to him, reminding him of things he didn't want to think about today, and his mood went dark. Money was Susan's bottom line, like it had been Alana's. In a different way, of course. One was personal, one was professional. But there wasn't so much distance between what was different and what was the same. *Money*. Wasn't that just the crux of a whole lot of problems?

He hadn't spoken a word in several minutes. One moment he was friendly and chatty, trying to challenge her and best her, which she actually liked. Then the next he was totally quiet, sitting under a black cloud. The scowl line between his eyes was so deep it aged him a dozen years. "I was wondering," she began, then glanced over to see if he was even listening, "if I could go back on duty for the night shift, after I've had a rest? Since I'm here to work, there's no point in my doing nothing until tomorrow. So, if you need—"

"We always *need*," he snapped, cutting her off. "And that's the problem. Too much need. Too few resources. People die because of it, but nobody cares except the people who can't do anything to solve the problem. And what Ridgeway will do to Kahawaii won't solve the problem because the resources won't make it to the people who need them most."

So it was back to that. She wasn't surprised by his mood, but she was put off by it. He saw Ridgeway as one of the great evils of the world, she saw it as an opportunity, a good resource for a facility, like Kahawaii Clinic, that was struggling. But she was simply tired of arguing, and she wasn't about to let him take away the good feelings still lingering. So Susan pulled closer to the door, not exactly huddling against it but more leaning to get farther away from him, and stared out the window, contemplating leaving here again. Everything she did seemed to set him off, and that wasn't good for the clinic. If she had any sense, she'd make him pull over so she could get out, hike back to the clinic, get in her rental car, and get out of here. Go back to what she knew best and forget these few days and, in particular, these past hours had ever happened. Most of all, forget how good she'd felt doing minor medical care.

Except she wasn't a quitter. If she left here, Grant would believe that proved him right about Ridgeway Medical, that it was everything bad he thought it was. Well, she didn't want to give him that impression, or satisfaction. Besides, a part of her really did want him to see the takeover for what it was—a chance at growth and modernization. A better opportunity. Although she would admit that right now she wasn't sure how that would work out here because she was beginning to see his point of view in the kind of medicine he practiced. Saw it for him anyway. It did work here. Worked very well, and she admired that. Admired the simplicity of it, too.

Maybe she was even beginning to pull for Grant to find a way to keep his clinic. "Have you looked for outside funding sources?" she said, feeling a little disloyal to her Ridgeway obligations, but not so disloyal that she wouldn't offer Grant a smidgen of her business know-how. "Or thought of going to some kind of standardized charge? I know the appeal of taking pineapples in lieu of payment has a nice aesthetic appeal…"

"It's not for aesthetics," he said, his voice not so snappish now. "It's for a real problem…people who cannot afford to pay. They're proud. Won't take charity, and I want to protect their dignity. That was one of the primary goals of the clinic when Dr Kahawaii started it…true charity. And there's never been a reason to do anything differently. People are more likely to come round if they have something to offer in exchange, which is why we take pineapples, if that's all they have. And it's offset by the ones who do pay, and the ones who have insurance. It keeps our bottom line, as you call it, pretty lean, but we get by."

"But we live in a modern society, Grant. There's a better way, if you'd just consider it."

"Even people in a modern society can be poor. *And proud.* What you have here, Susan, isn't like Chicago, or Los Angeles. It isn't even like Honolulu. So many of the people here skirt between modern society and the old, traditional ways. They fish because they need to eat. Sure, some of them might have computers in their homes, but they also use the breadfruit growing on the tree right outside their doors as a staple in their diets. And in the summer, when it gets too hot, the ones who don't have air-conditioning go down to the beach and live. They camp there for days, or weeks, just to stay cooler. Kids go to school, adults go to college, it's not a primitive society by any means, but it's still a different reality than what most people expect. And it's part of the heritage we don't want to let go of."

"And there's no reaching out for help for the clinic? Does the heritage you're trying to preserve preclude that?" She wasn't trying to be contentious. More like she wanted to understand. She herself didn't live in a simple way, and Grant did. They were both highly educated, yet she could see him camping on the beach for days or weeks, while she was totally dependent on the amenities of a nice hotel. It was a different reality and in a way she envied him the heritage that allowed it. It gave him a keen sense of purpose. He knew who he was.

"Not preclude it. And, believe me, I've tried to reach out. But I don't practice the latest in modern medicine here and so much of the outside funding comes with strings attached that won't work for Kahawaii, if Kahawaii is to work for its patients." He drew in a deep breath, shrugging some of the tension out of his shoulders and neck. "My knowledge is fine, Susan. As up to date as anybody's, I suppose. I study, I keep up with all the latest advances. But none of that makes a lot of difference if my patient refuses to come to the clinic under any circumstances. In your world, she'd be forgotten. In my world, she's not. I'll make that drive. And that's the difference between your medicine and mine. But, unfortunately, time is money, and in terms of what Ridgeway Medical will expect, spending two hours to visit Moana isn't productive." He finally relaxed into his seat, the frown on his face melting away. "Unless you need a new shirt."

"I could use a shirt," she said, glad his anger had finally passed.

"Especially if you're going to stay for five more days. You *are* going to stay, aren't you?"

"Are you sure that's what you want, Grant? I know it's not easy for you, having me here as a constant reminder of what's about to happen, and, believe it or not, I really don't want to disrupt you, don't want to cause problems." A little stir of disappointment over the prospect of not spending a few more days in paradise swept through her. Susan Ridgeway Cantwell, whose biggest adventure so far had been collecting seashells and lounging on a beach towel, reading romance novels, liked what she was doing here and she didn't want to give it up yet.

But she would, because at heart she was a real doctor, not just one who sat in an admin seat. She really did want what was best for the patients here. And for Grant.

Of course, part of what she was feeling was that stir she got from Grant, and she wasn't going to try and fool herself about it. She was attracted to him, which was crazy. It wouldn't… couldn't go anywhere. In fact, it wouldn't even get started. She was the enemy, pure and simple. He couldn't perceive her any other way. Yet being around him made her feel…good. Confident. Important in a way Ridgeway didn't make her feel, like what she did here really mattered, even if it was only bandaging a scraped elbow or knee. "Because it wouldn't hurt my feelings if you didn't want—"

"I suggested, you agreed. That's still the deal," he interrupted, his voice serious. But the crinkle at the corners of his eyes said otherwise. "There's no need to change it, unless you want to."

"I don't want to," she murmured, feeling more at ease now than she had been in ages. And the reason she felt so relaxed…yes, she was looking forward to the medical duty. That was part of it. The other part had something to do with the attractive force that swirled all around him. Being around that made her feel like *she* was swirling, too.

# CHAPTER SIX

THE ride along the dirt road was beautiful, and a bit jarring in places. In her world she didn't take to dirt roads too often, but with the spectacular view of the lush tropical greens dotting the austere mountains, the little bumps she incurred were well worth it. She'd never given much thought to Hawaii, other than its beaches, but it was rugged, wild, full of jungles and places that looked totally unexplored. Life took place on the edges of the island, but the interior was so vast, and so stunningly unexpected. And after nearly twenty minutes of bumping along a dusty, overgrown little road, not meeting a single other person or car along the way, she was glad when Grant pulled off into a small clearing on the side and turned off the engine. She needed a stretch, and she also wanted to have a closer look at some of the beautiful wild orchids she'd spotted in patches every now and then along the road. This was a perfect spot as there was a pretty little clump of white orchids growing up the side of a palm tree so close to where he'd stopped she could almost reach out the window and pick them.

She needed to walk off some of her road-weariness, too. City girl, she thought as she stepped down to the ground, then turned slowly to take in the entire landscape. "It's beautiful," she said. "I never expected it to be so…"

"Unspoiled," he supplied.

She nodded. "That's a good word for it. I'm surprised the tourists haven't made it this far into the interior."

"They want the beaches, and the conveniences. Back here it isn't convenient."

"Except you do know your way around back here, don't you?" Alone in paradise with him did unnerve her just the slightest. And not in a bad way.

He chuckled. "You don't get anything like this in Dallas. Does it make you nervous?"

"Not nervous so much as overwhelmed. I'm used to…buildings. People. Noise." She drew in a deep breath of the pure, clean air and let it trickle slowly into her lungs. Back home in Dallas the air was so thick with humidity it was hard to breathe. There were days when it felt like she was fighting to drag in the next breath, fighting to force it down all the way into her lungs. And here breathing felt so…healthy.

If she wasn't careful, this could become addictive. "I'm glad we stopped here," she admitted, walking over to the massive palm tree to sniff the orchid growing in perfect symbiosis with it.

"We didn't stop, Kekoa," he said, slinging his canvas medical bag over his shoulder. "In fact, we're only just beginning."

The first few minutes of their hike was pleasant, taking in all the sights, things she'd never seen before. She asked him about various flowers and plants as they came across them, and stopped occasionally to watch an exotic bird. She could almost imagine getting lost in such an exquisite paradise and living there happily ever after. A fairy tale in the making for someone who believed in fairy tales. She didn't, but she wanted to.

Once, Grant stopped, then indicated for her to do the same. "Do you smell it?" he asked.

Susan cocked her head inquisitively, inhaled deeply, and concentrated on the pleasant scent. "It's almost sweet, and a little pungent." She wasn't sure what fragrance wafted in on the breeze.

"Yellow ginger."

"Just growing wild?"

"Ginger, eucalyptus… It's used in traditional Hawaiian medicine."

She took in another deep breath. "Are there still traditional healers here?"

"We have a few left, but most people now prefer modern medicine. It's a shame," he said, distracted for a moment by a mynah bird flying overhead, calling down to them in a cackling laugh. "A lost art that still could have a place in a medical practice if we'd let it in."

*Which Ridgeway wouldn't do.* He didn't say the words, but they were implied. That snapped her out of her mellowing mood, setting her right back on edge. "You're a trained physician. Your clinic may not be ultramodern by some standards, but you've got to know that treating a respiratory ailment with antibiotics is preferable to having your patient inhale eucalyptus."

"Is it? In what tradition, Susan? Where I live it can go either way. And to be honest, if I were the one suffering from a respiratory ailment, I'd rather try eucalyptus first, before putting antibiotics into my body. It's healthier. Much less invasive."

"You don't use eucalyptus at Kahawaii, do you?"

"I have. And I would do it again if I thought a little *natural* medicine was warranted. It's about what's best for the patient, not what's best for the medical institution."

So they were back to that. Going round in circles, always ending up where they'd started. "Without the medical institution, there's no treatment for the patient, no matter what that treatment is. You've *got* to take into consideration what's best for the medical institution, too, and I don't understand how you can't see that!"

Rather than continuing the argument, Grant laughed aloud. "That little frown line between your eyes is getting deeper. Out here, we don't allow that. Worrying and stressing so much isn't healthy."

"So what would you prescribe to cure me of that, Doctor?" she asked, trying to sound serious about it even though a smile was pulling at her lips. Grant was coaxing her back into a good mood and she couldn't help it. "Eucalyptus or yellow ginger?"

"Actually, eucalyptus is very relaxing. And not as overpowering as a sedative, which is what *your* type of medicine might have me prescribe for you—a sedative."

Well, she did admire his persistence. Grant Makela had the strongest sense of purpose she'd ever seen in anybody, and she did admire that. So much so that the part of her that wanted him to keep his clinic was growing. "Actually, you're wrong. I've been known to indulge in a little aromatherapy for relaxation purposes from time to time."

"You're a stubborn woman, Kekoa. You don't give in. I think I like that in you."

"What does *kekoa* mean?" she asked. "You called me that a little while ago."

"It means courageous."

"But I'm not."

He laughed. "Do you always belittle yourself that way? Somebody pays you a compliment and your first response is to rebuff it?"

"Just trying to keep things honest. I'm not courageous."

"Then how would you describe yourself?"

"Hardworking."

"Yes, I'm sure you are."

"And honest."

He shook his head. "I think you're trying to avoid honesty. Because you are *kekoa,* even if you don't want to see it."

"Possibly what you want to see is not what exists. Believe me, I know how easy it is to totally avoid reality and replace it with whatever works best for the situation." The story of her life much more than she cared to admit. Her marriage, her job as of late—she'd replaced the reality of both with what had seemed to work best at the time.

"Or what exists is not what you want to see," he tossed out for her consideration. Grant snapped a wild orchid off its vine and handed it to her. "Tuck it behind your right ear if you're available, your left if you're taken." Then he waited for her. Rather than picking available or taken, however, she held the orchid to her nose for a moment, enjoying the sweet scent, then she dropped it on the ground.

"Neither one," she said, regretting the choice. But it was the honest one, because that's what she'd chosen for her life.

"Well, then, you're correct about one thing. Sometimes it *is* easier to avoid the reality and replace it with whatever works best for the situation."

As they continued their journey off-trail, Susan forced herself to think about things other than the orchid she'd left behind or Grant's perceptions of her. That was all clutter, more distraction, which she didn't need from him as she seemed to be doing a good job of distracting herself. "Does your patient, Moana, have to come this way to get to her house? Because if she's elderly, isn't this awfully strenuous for her?" Susan asked, as she pulled away from Grant long enough to stop and look at a peculiar tree with myriad thick roots either growing up from the ground or dropping down from the limbs, she couldn't tell which. One tree could make a small forest unto itself, and the one she spotted off in the distance must have had a hundred trunklike roots. It was so vast it might have been possible to get lost in the growth of a single tree, and that reminded her of Ridgeway Medical. One company with so much growth it, too, held the possibility of getting lost in all its growth. The way Grant feared Kahawaii would. Maybe his fear had merit, she thought as she studied all the codependent roots. They were beautiful on their own, and had great purpose, but if the trunk of the tree didn't exist, neither would those roots.

Noticing Susan's curiosity, Grant explained, "It's called a banyan, and that one's small compared to some. Once they start growing they never seem to stop."

Again, like Ridgeway Medical.

"And Moana," he continued. "She's hearty, and I think she probably could take this trail if she wanted, but this is the long way to her house, going up the back route. You can drive straight to her door, but I like to come this way."

"You have time to take a detour?" she asked. Of course, that was the administrator in her coming out again. She couldn't help it. Somewhere in the back of her mind efficiency matters were always clicking away, and this little trek seemed such a huge waste of time as it wasn't leading them straight to their patient. Although she *was* enjoying it, and there was something to be said for taking some time for that. Still, she felt inner conflict. Her natural inclination was fighting to get out and slap down the pure enjoyment of doing something spontaneous in a life that never allowed in a shred of spontaneity.

"Life isn't much fun without the detours," he said, as if reading her thoughts. "They're good for reducing stress, lowering blood pressure, if you want to be practical about it. It you don't, that straight journey from place to place can be pretty boring and it's the detours winding in and out that make it more interesting."

"And less productive," she challenged, still fighting the devil in her that didn't approve of this foolishness. The truth was, she wanted to relax and enjoy herself. She just couldn't.

"Have you ever seen a bird-of-paradise in the wild, Susan? It's a beautiful, unusual flower you'll never find along that straight line, and to walk right by it and not take the detour to stop and admire it would be such a waste." He pulled back a clump of ferns, and there, nestled behind them was, indeed, a bird-of-paradise plant.

It was odd, almost out of place there, standing alone. Like she was. But it held a certain exotic grace in its position she admired and even envied. "I'll admit the flowers are wonderful," she said on a wistful sigh, tiring of her own argument now. It was all she had, though. "But life isn't about hunting down the exotic bird-of-paradise, and you're only doing this to prove a point—that you know what I need better than I do."

"Is that what you think I'm doing?"

"Aren't you? We could be on our way back to the clinic by now, but we're wandering down a beautiful path without an aim."

"Don't be so stodgy, Susan. There's always an aim."

Yes, there was, but not always one she could allow herself. "Then let me rephrase that. Without a *valid* aim. Hiking out in the middle of a workday to see a bird-of-paradise isn't a valid aim." She didn't want to make this more than it was, but taking off like they were, in the middle of the day, could become habit-forming. All the arguments for or against making house calls aside, this little trip couldn't be justified. Worse than that, she was thoroughly enjoying every unjustified moment of it.

"Then how about we just say that this isn't about what you

need, that it's about what I need? Would that work better for you? Absolve you of all those guilty feelings you're struggling with?"

"Who says I have guilty feelings?" she snapped, not because of the situation so much as because he was so good at reading her. Grant's sentiment might be nice, but the more she meandered away from her own life, the more she realized she wasn't suited for anything else. No getting away from who she was. That was definitely not *kekoa,* which made her angry. And sad for all the things she would never have.

Rather than answering, Grant grabbed Susan's hand and pulled her along again. As he did, a tingly jolt of electricity crept up her arm—one that shocked her so quickly and sharply she wondered if he'd felt it, too.

"You…um…you went to medical school on the mainland," she said, grappling for words as she deliberately changed the subject. She didn't want to fight with him any more, didn't want him taking wild guesses about her either. Time to go impersonal. Rein in this conversation and talk about things that meant nothing.

"In California."

"Would you ever go back…to practice, maybe?"

"After Ridgeway buys Kahawaii Clinic and fires me? Is that what you mean?"

Susan braced herself with a deep breath. "You don't make simple conversation very easy, Grant."

"But, according to your standards, isn't simple conversation a waste of time?"

Susan pulled away from him and stopped dead in the middle of the trail. "Pick a position, Grant. Business or pleasure? You get after me when I wander back to business, yet when I try to make a little personal chat, you throw me right back to the side of business. So, you choose and I'll oblige."

His eyes sparkled with amusement. This little back and forth between them, if it hadn't been over something so very important, could have been downright sexy. Normally she hated to spar with anyone, but sparring with Grant was different. He turned it into something almost sexy.

Grant straightened his shoulders, giving her a long, leisurely stare before he began. "After about four or five days away from here I start feeling…I think the best way to describe it is crowded. I do go down to Costa Rica a couple of times a year, usually two weeks each trip, with a volunteer medical group, but when I'm there I'm on the edge of a jungle where we set up practice, so that's different. It's nice. Easy. A lot like it is here. Anyplace else, though…" He faked a cringe. "Leave me out of it. I know where I belong!"

And she didn't, but she didn't believe that's what he was trying to imply. To be honest, she envied him that sureness in his life. "I think it would be nice to be attached to a place…have some kind of stability, the way you do. For me, home is just a condo. I'm not even settled in enough to have any pictures on the wall. And I travel so much that about half my nights are spent in a hotel somewhere. Sometimes when I wake up I'm not even sure where I am. My secretary has to call me in the mornings to remind me." Finally, a better conversation. One that didn't evoke so many emotions and senseless ideas.

"How long have you lived in your condo?"

"In that particular condo, about a year now. It's closer to the office than the one I used to have. Shorter travel time back and forth. Makes my time more productive." The topic was getting dangerously close to work again. It seemed that even when she tried to veer off course she wasn't very good at it.

"And there's nothing personal in it to make it comfortable for you?"

"Comfort's relative to what you need. As I'm not there much, I don't need much." A fact that actually sounded detached. But, honestly, she didn't need the homey, cozy feel that Grant had here on the island.

"Well, I'll admit I don't have much of a home myself, but what I have suits me pretty well. Nothing extravagant, but I'm comfortable." He pushed back an overgrown clump of vines and pulled her off the path through a thicket that didn't seem to have been disturbed by civilization at all.

What was amazing to her was how willingly she went with him. This was so far removed from anything she ever did and she wondered if a deep, unexplored yearning might be surfacing in her. Given her restless feelings lately, nothing would surprise her. But she couldn't survive and thrive in a place like this, as Grant did. Could she?

That thought flittered in and right back out. She might be craving something different, but she was far too practical to settle into something this different. It was fine for a holiday, and even for a few days of work, but that was it. She had to be pragmatic about it at some point.

Pragmatic in paradise. How stodgy was that?

"When you get into areas such as this," Grant continued, "out of the city, life is casual. Values aren't taken for granted. We don't put as much stock in the things we own as we do in enjoying our lives."

"And it works," Susan said, almost amazed. In her world, it was all about what you owned. For heaven's sake, she and her father owned a private jet. Life was never casual for someone with a private jet. And for her, the value of life was measured in the number of business deals on the table at any given time, and in the number of properties they owned. She wasn't even sure she'd know how to be casual if she had the chance.

"Yes, it works in my life. But not in your life?"

"My life is complicated." That was putting it mildly. Her life was a jumble of business deals, one after another.

"You don't sound happy about that."

"That's complicated, too." Especially right now. Although she wasn't about to ruin such a lovely day talking about all that. It just depressed her, and she didn't want to be depressed. "So, when will we get to Moana's?" she asked, trying not to dwell on the complications of her real life.

"In due time. We could take that straight line you prefer, but you'd miss all this, and even in your complicated life, Susan, there are some things you shouldn't miss."

She opened her mouth to argue again, but it was gone from her now. Instead, she merely stepped up alongside him when he motioned for her to do so, and as she did, realized he had won all the arguments. Looking out over the little bluff on which they were standing, she saw a nearly hidden waterfall cascading down over a craggy rock formation on the other side of the most pristine, clear pool of water she'd ever seen. The falls were splashing lazily down into it, and on all sides there plants and tropical flowers so brilliantly colored she had to blink twice to be sure it was real. Grant was so right about this…about her…it nearly took her breath away. He did know what was best for her, as this was something she would have refused to come see, yet she shouldn't have missed it. "Thank you," she said simply, as she went ahead of him, taking in everything…studying it, memorizing it. Cherishing it. "This is amazing."

"It's called 'Aka 'Aka Falls, which means Laughing Falls, because when you stand at the top and call down, the echo sounds like laughing. Moana lives just on the other side, and we could have driven to her door or walked through what is practically her front yard. I thought you might enjoy the front yard, even though it's not on your schedule."

She wanted to argue that she didn't always live by her schedule, but she did. Grant won that one without her saying a word. For this moment, she wanted to be more like him. Casual. Easy. At peace with life, the way he was. Taking time for side trips like this. She turned back to face him. "You brought me here just so I could see this, didn't you?"

"More like experience it. It's calm here. Peaceful. And you're not, Susan. You're stressed out, you frown too much. This is where I like to come when I need to think, or relax, or simply get away from everything that's bothering me for a little while. My mother used to bring me here when I was a boy. She'd pack a lunch and we'd come for the afternoon just to avoid the realities we had to face in our everyday lives."

Grant stepped back up to Susan, took her hand and led her closer to the pool, to a clearing in the plants where there was a little outcrop of flat rocks. She imagined this was the exact spot where he'd spent those lazy afternoons with his mother, having their picnics on those very rocks. "We never had time for picnics. My father was always driven to work, and there wasn't anything left over for…anything frivolous."

"Am I hearing some bitterness?"

Susan shook her head. "Not bitterness. When that's what your life is about, it's all you know, and there's no need to be bitter. You can't miss what you don't know."

"Then I think we should have a bit of one of those afternoons you missed." With that, he bent down and unlaced one of his hiking shoes, then pulled it off, along with his sock.

"What are you doing?" she gasped.

Rather than answering, he merely grinned at her and started on his other shoe.

Wading. That's what Susan thought. They were going wading, and she was suddenly excited by the prospect of doing it, of taking off her own shoes and engaging in something so totally uncharacteristic of her. Trying to remember a time that she might have done something like this, Susan sat down on the ground and pulled off her first shoe. She was fully involved in tugging off her second one before she noticed that Grant had gone beyond the shedding of his shoes and was in the process of unzipping his khaki shorts. "You're not going to…? You really don't expect me to… You're really not going to do that, are you?" she gasped, as his khakis slipped to the ground.

She stared for a moment, not at all shy about taking in his nicely bronzed, half-naked form. Gorgeous. Totally gorgeous. All the *if onlys* crept in fast.

"Just going for a swim," he said, grinning down at her. "Feel free to join me."

She shook her head, snapping herself out of the moment. "I didn't bring my swimsuit."

"Spoken like a woman who doesn't know how to relax and go with the moment."

"Suit yourself. But I'm not getting naked and swimming with you. No arguments, Grant. You can pull me out of my comfort zone, but not that far out."

This was definitely getting too personal, too close to everything she didn't allow, and for a moment she wondered if this was merely his way of trying to distract her from what was bound to be inevitable. Would he go so far as to seduce her, hoping that would somehow have a bearing on the outcome of the deal for the clinic? "You know what, Grant? Why don't you point me in the direction of Moana's house and I'll go on up and see her. You said she prefers women to make the house call anyway, so I'll do that and you can stay here and swim to your heart's content."

"You'll get lost. It gets a little tricky up around the bend."

"I'm not stupid. Give me the directions and I'll be fine."

"There's that frown again." He reached over and stroked the spot between her eyes with his thumb. "Too deep, too serious."

"None of your business!" she snapped, yanking away from his touch, wishing now that she'd simply gone back to her own life instead of trying to fit into this one. Grant wasn't really suggesting anything untoward. Certainly a little swim *could be* part of the whole casual package that went along with his lifestyle, but the problem was, once she gave in to it, that could make it all the more difficult to do what she would eventually have to do if Ridgeway took over his clinic. Technically, she would be his boss, which made this cozy little scene unfolding right now totally unprofessional. "I'm not like you, Grant," she cried. "And bringing me out here and telling me to relax isn't going to change who, or what, I am. It's not going to affect the outcome of the business deal either."

"Do you think that's what this is about?"

"I don't know what this is about, and I don't want to know." She gestured to the pool, the flowers, and the scarlet and black *iiwi* bird sipping nectar from a fiery red *ohia lehua* blossom nearby. "This was supposed to be about six days of escaping my situation but not about escaping who I am. I'm the medical director for Ridgeway, one who has a frown line that may seem too deep and serious to you, and if your intention is solely about helping me relax, I appreciate the concern, but taking off my clothes and going into the water with you isn't going to miraculously erase the frown, my obligations, or your situation."

"So it's better not to relax at all? It's better to sit here and be everything you are back in Texas rather than experience the moment when you're in it?"

"It's better not to tempt myself with the moment," she said, fighting hard not to sound sad. Which she was now.

He held out his hand to her. "You don't have to get naked, and this isn't about business. I'm not trying to sway you in the way Ridgeway may take over the clinic."

Was he really this genuine? She wanted him to be. For all the problems they were destined to have between them, she really did want Grant to be who he seemed to be. But in business transactions people put on amazing fronts and pretenses to win what they wanted, and a business deal did await them after all.

Grant was endearing, though, darned persistent, and sexier than any man had a right to be. That's how he seemed to her, and that's how she wanted him to be. She felt herself totally swaying with that sentiment. Why did he do that to her? How could he have that power?

"Ten minutes, Susan," he said, sticking his hand right back out to her.

"I know. Ten minutes that will transform my life. That's what you're offering me, isn't it?"

He laughed. "Well, that's a mighty tall order. How about something smaller, like ten minutes that will transform your day? We can start there, with the small steps, and leave the rest of it alone."

"And what if I don't trust you?"

"What if I don't trust you?" he countered.

"But I've been honest with you. You know who I am, and what I may have to do in the very near future."

"I've been honest with you, too. I've told you how I feel, told you that you're making a mistake, told you that what you have in mind for Kahawaii Clinic isn't in the best interests of its patients, and that's all honest, Susan. That's as honest as it gets, and that's the only thing important here. So why wouldn't I be honest about my intentions to get you into the pool?"

"Ten minutes." Giving in to his power of persuasion—*she wasn't kidding herself, she was giving in to his potency*—she took his hand and stood. "Damn your logic, anyway, Grant Makela. I don't want to do this."

He arched his eyebrows, his eyes underneath them twinkling with laughter. "Then we won't for any longer than *twenty* minutes."

"You're pushing it," she warned. This man was totally irresistible, and she had a feeling he knew it. More than that, he used it to his advantage.

"Ten minutes is never enough, Susan. But I'll let you make the call after ten minutes." Rather than standing there watching her decide whether to do this in full dress or give in to an unrestrained little impulse and strip to her panties and bra, he turned and walked away. She assumed he was respecting her privacy anyway, which she did appreciate, as doing something so unpredictable certainly wasn't her nature.

"No one's going to find us here, are they?" she called after him. "I mean, it's just going to be the two of us here, isn't it?"

She waited for an answer, but when none came she debated the swimming situation for another minute before she finally decided to go for it. Not all the way, of course. So, while she was still brave enough to do this, and second thoughts weren't beginning to pummel her, she pulled off the clinic garb she'd worn—floral-print shirt, blue cotton scrub pants—then ran as fast as she could to the water's edge. Once there, she looked around for Grant, but he was nowhere to be seen.

"I'm going in," she called out, hoping to draw a response from him. But for the second time she heard no reply. So she waded in ankle-deep, relishing the coolness of the water coming up over her feet. Then she took another step, and another, until she was in up to her knees. Funny how on all those mornings on the beach she'd never gone in over her ankles, typical of her over-cautious outlook, yet look at her now, wading in further and further…figuratively as well as literally. "Okay, where are you?" she called. "You were the one who wanted me to do this, so aren't you going to come and swim with me?"

Again, he didn't answer, and this time a little tingle of nervousness crept up her spine. Was this merely a game after all? Sway her to do something she wouldn't normally do then go off somewhere to watch her make a fool of herself? Would he get a kick out of seeing his future boss behaving so stupidly? Had his intention all along been about getting her out of her clothes, into the water, out of her total comfort zone, for some scheming purpose?

Common sense slapped her like a swift, open hand, the old caution returning with a vengeance. What had she been thinking anyway, doing something like this? It was crazy. Out of character. Worst of all, she'd believed she could actually put aside everything she was for a little while and be this other person. Grant had convinced her of that and, foolishly, she'd believed him.

Angry with herself for being so gullible about his good looks and charm, Susan spun around, ready to head back to the shore, back to her clothes, back to Grant's car. No more of this nonsense. She knew where she belonged, and it was time to return there. Forget the lunacy that spending a few days as a doctor in paradise would make any difference to anyone. It hadn't to Ryan Harris, and there was nothing more to say.

Sloshing through the water, Susan was almost back to the edge when she heard a shout from somewhere behind her. It was Grant, calling her name. But she wouldn't turn round. To do that would be to give in to the folly. So she continued, and just as she stepped onto dry land, she heard him again.

"Susan! Up here!"

His voice was far away, which did catch her interest enough to spin her round to have a look. But she couldn't see him…not in the water, not on the shore.

"Susan…"

She glanced up. Screened her eyes with one hand. Squinted into the sun. Gasped when she finally saw him perched on a cliff just above the waterfall. He was waving to her.

She didn't wave back to acknowledge him, though. Rather, she stood there, focused on what he was about to do, watching him move closer to the cliff's edge, watching him pose above it, then… Grant waved at her once more then dove off the cliff, his body bending into a perfect jackknife at first, then lengthening into a muscular birdlike creature sailing gracefully through the air, angling straight at the water, until he slipped into the pool, head first, causing barely a ripple.

The breath caught in Susan's throat at first as she grasped the pure beauty of his lean body. Beautiful form. Stunning. Another Adonis, only this one of the cliffs. Normally, she never even noticed men. And here she was with two of them capturing a little more than only her fancy.

But she had to be careful. She knew that. This paradise of Grant's was dangerous, and standing here on the edge of it in her panties and bra was putting more ideas in her head than she realized she should have. So, before he'd made his way to shore, she scrambled back into her clothes, took the keys to his Jeep from his pocket, picked up the medical bags and ran back along the trail they'd taken to get here. A little later, in Grant's Jeep, she pulled up to the front of the little house at the end of the road on which they'd been traveling, only to find Grant lounging on a chair on the front porch. "Look, Grant, I've been rethinking my decision to stay here another few days," she said. "I don't think it's going to work out the way I thought it would."

"Because I dove off a cliff?" he asked. "Or because you didn't?"

"I don't belong here."

"So your intention is what? Changing Kahawaii into a place where you do belong?" He stood up and took the bag containing the canned corned beef. "You know what, Susan? I think you're scared because you're realizing that you could belong here." Drops of water glistened through the strands of his coal-black hair as he pushed a few stray locks back from his face. "Maybe even want to."

"What I want is to get this house call over with."

"Oh, I'm sure you do. Then you'll call your superiors and tell them to write new Ridgeway policy, one where house calls are not allowed in the future."

She glared pure fire at him for a moment, but rather than responding she pushed around him, practically knocking him aside on her way to the door.

"You're a good doctor, Susan. And what you're seeing here is going to rub off on you. You know that, don't you? When you go back to Ridgeway Medical, and make your recommendations, if you suggest doing anything differently than what we already do here, you'll be a hypocrite because you know what Kahawaii needs."

"And I know what Ridgeway needs, too," she said almost under her breath, as a kind-faced, gray-haired little lady opened the door to her and invited her inside. Before going in, she turned back to Grant and snatched the bag of canned meat from his hand. "And just so you'll know, Grant, I don't have to *call* my superiors. I *am* the superior. My maiden name is Ridgeway."

# CHAPTER SEVEN

WELL, he hadn't seen that one coming. Susan *Ridgeway* Cantwell. He'd spent an afternoon and a night kicking himself over it. Probably should have been packing his clothes, sending out his résumé on a job search.

To Susan's credit, she'd risen above that blazingly awful moment between them, hadn't mentioned a word of it since she'd come back to Kahawaii and put in two shifts, back to back. He'd worked a shift, then lost a good night's sleep, alternately pacing the floor and searching the Internet for anything that could help him wrestle the clinic away from…well, that would be Susan, wouldn't it? In the moments when he hadn't been preoccupied with the obvious, he'd spent the time wondering why he'd thought that a little side trip away from the clinic could change matters between them.

Actually, it had, hadn't it? It had made everything worse.

What the hell had he been thinking, coaxing the owner of Ridgeway Medical to have an almost-naked swim with him? If he'd scripted a way to kill his chances of winning Kahawaii, he couldn't have done a better job.

Still, there was something about Susan that made her seem so close to understanding the things he knew and believed and trusted, and that wasn't wishful thinking. It was there. He saw it in the way she took care of her patients, in the way she related to the other staff members…well, except him. She hadn't spoken a word to him since she'd entered Moana's house.

So what was it about Susan that had him in this state? Something other than the fact that in the very near future she would, most likely, have the power to control his professional future? Was it her vulnerability? It had to be more than the challenge of cracking her tough exterior, and while the thought had crossed his mind that sleeping with her could be nice, it wasn't that either. If he did want to sleep with someone, he'd definitely pick someone easier than Susan. So, what the hell was it making him act this way?

Given his recent lousy track record with women, it was probably better that he didn't answer that question. Not even to himself. But he didn't have to. The answer was as glaringly obvious as the ocean waves he rode every morning. Future boss or not, he was attracted to Susan. Maybe even a little more than attracted. She was gorgeous, and he loved the challenge of her. Plus, she was smart, and she was a good doctor. Tie all that up and it was a great package. The problem was, when he opened that package, it would explode. Blow up and ruin everything he'd planned for as long as he could remember.

"Do I have a way of picking them or what?" he muttered, as he plodded into the pediatric ward. If there was a woman within a thousand miles of him who would be the worst possible choice, he'd find her. And he had, twice now. First Alana. Now little Miss Corporate Executive, who attracted him like no other woman ever had, including Alana, which was a sure disaster in the making. If it went any further than his own muddled mind, that was. "So, 'Eleu," he said to the black-haired, dark-eyed little girl, the only child in the four-bed ward. "Are you being good today?"

He knew 'Eleu, knew her grandfather. They were neighbors, in fact. Lived on the same road a few houses down from his. Good people, and having a tough time of it now. Tough times ahead, too, he was afraid. "Are you doing what the nurses tell you to do?" Grant persisted, trying to sound cheerful, even though he ached for the child.

'Eleu, a normally precocious and bright little girl, looked up at Grant for a moment, her eyes so far away and sad it broke his heart. She'd spoken precious few words since she'd been in Kahawaii, almost a week now. Normally, it was a polite and very timid "Yes" or "No." That was all anybody had gotten out of her so far. Something about the trauma of capsizing in an outrigger canoe and being swarmed by sharks tended to do that to a child. And what she'd seen…

Her grandfather, Ka Nui, had been critically injured, and had been flown directly to a hospital in Honolulu, one more able to treat major trauma. He'd barely survived the attack and the ensuing flight, although word from the hospital that morning had been that he was recovering slowly—unfortunately, without his left leg. In addition, he'd suffered a slight stroke from the blood loss of his injury, which had resulted in some physical impairment for him to overcome once he got used to the fact that he no longer had two legs. So much to deal with for a man his age…somewhere in his mid-seventies. So many traumas for anybody to deal with.

And all that left 'Eleu, who was already an orphan being raised by her grandfather, alone here in the clinic. Alone and frightened. She was recovering well from her own wounds, which weren't serious—several deep bite marks on both legs, but nothing that went as deep as the bone. For a seven-year-old girl who'd already lived through so much other tragedy in the loss of her parents when she'd been a baby, this was a horrible complication in the poor child's life. Luckily, no surgery had been required on her wounds. Not so many stitches either. Even now, her only real course of treatment was a round of antibiotics and clean bandages every day. So the prognosis for 'Eleu was good. Physically, anyway, as he suspected her worst injury was the emotional trauma she'd suffered. Bad weather springing up, huge waves capsizing the outrigger as a result, sharks swarming in for the kill, then suddenly all the things a little girl had always counted on as safe had not been.

Life was so damned tenuous sometimes, Grant thought as he handed 'Eleu a lollipop. Tenuous and unpredictable. And, as often, unfair.

The girl took the candy from him, and instead of unwrapping it eagerly, the way most children would do, she simply placed it on the bedside table with the other lollipops he'd brought her. *"Mahalo nui loa,"* she said, then looked away. *Thank you very much.* Her voice had been so quiet he'd scarcely heard it.

"Want to go for a walk?" he asked. "You haven't been out of this room for a whole week now and the fresh air will do you good."

She didn't respond, the way she hadn't responded to almost anything else he'd said this past week. Which was why he hadn't expected anything different from her this time. The truth was, he was getting concerned about her withdrawal. The pediatrician who came in twice a week had said that she would come around in her own good time, that children processed events differently than adults did and dealt with the aftermath differently, too. Dr Chen had been very specific in instructing Grant not to worry about the way 'Eleu was reacting now, that she would eventually become more responsive, but not until her mind was ready to deal with what she'd gone through, to put some sense to it in a way she could understand and deal with.

The orders Dr Chen had left had been for routine medical care and as much human intervention as could be managed, but not to force 'Eleu to do anything she didn't want to. That's what Grant was doing now, and feeling pretty damned inadequate about it. "I have a wheelchair waiting," he said, to let the girl know she wouldn't be expected to walk. With her injuries, it was too soon for that.

But 'Eleu, who'd been studying him in quick, almost unnoticeable flashes, taking brief peeks at him from under her thick, dark lashes, folded her arms across her chest and looked away, indicating she wasn't interested in anything he had to offer.

So now the dilemma. To use a little gentle persuasion on her? Or to allow her to have her own way, no matter how long that took? To be honest, he hadn't figured out what to do with 'Eleu yet. When he'd called Chen a while ago, Chen's advice had been to use common sense and allow each situation to dictate itself, which was no help to him whatsoever. On a better note, Chen had promised Grant he'd come by tomorrow for a quick check, which was good, but that didn't take care of the situation today. And right now common sense wasn't giving him anything to work with.

He was torn between wanting to take 'Eleu out for a little while in the hope that doing something different might make her feel better, and causing more emotional damage if she'd developed some sort of security attachment to where she was now. He didn't want to rip her away from her only constant, and cause even further damage. "Tell me what to do, 'Eleu," he said. "I really think it would be nice to go outside for a walk, and I think you'd enjoy that. But I don't want to scare you. So can you help me out here? Tell me what you'd rather do than take a walk? Maybe go to the recreation room and watch a movie? We have a nice library of them here. Or draw pictures?" If she'd asked him to stand on his head and sing her a song he'd have done it, he was that desperate.

But she didn't do so much as blink at him. Instead, she kept her head turned away, staring off at nothing.

"Doc Etana," Susan said from the doorway, where'd she been watching the exchange for the past couple of minutes. Her first words to him since the day before. "How could you possibly ask a young lady to go out for a walk, the way 'Eleu looks?"

Grant spun around, blinking in surprise. So did 'Eleu, for that matter.

"Her hair isn't combed, and that hospital gown…no young lady would be caught going anywhere in something like that. It's awful, isn't it, 'Eleu?"

The girl did respond with a tentative nod, but that was all.

"Well, I think she needs a wardrobe change and some attention to her hair, as well as perfumed lotion and maybe even a little lipstick," Susan continued.

'Eleu suddenly shook her head, rather adamantly.

"No lotion?" Susan asked, tossing Grant a slight smile.

"Lipstick," the child said very quietly. "*Kupuna kane* won't let me. I'm not old enough."

A smile crept to Grant's lips as he gave Susan an approving nod. "Her grandfather," he explained.

"Well, then, what *kupuna kane* says goes. No lipstick." Susan turned toward Grant. "Now, if you'll excuse us, we have some work to do here." She turned immediately back to 'Eleu and held out a bottle of shampoo. "It's my favorite—jasmine."

'Eleu took a sniff, then nodded. But she still didn't smile. Which was fine. It was a step in the right direction, and Grant was pleased. He was pleased, too, that Susan had finally spoken to him, even if only for the benefit of a patient.

Neither Susan nor 'Eleu noticed Grant as he left the room, happy with what he'd just witnessed. An amazing transformation. Good doctoring wasn't all about dispensing medicine. Sometimes it was more about the human touch than anything else, and in that, no one was better than Susan. He envied her that, and wondered why someone with that kind of talent kept herself chained to a desk, even if she was a Ridgeway. For almost a week now he'd tried three or four times a day to get through to 'Eleu, to find something that interested her, and had failed miserably. But in a matter of seconds Susan had succeeded. That was a rare gift and, to be honest, he was surprised that Miss Corporate Executive had it in her. Surprised, but satisfied. Especially for 'Eleu.

Of course, it was all short-term, wasn't it? And if he wasn't careful about the way he acted around Susan, even shorter than he'd planned, given the way he'd let things get out of control yesterday.

As Susan continued working with 'Eleu, Grant went to his quarters, splashed a little water on his face and picked up the phone to make a call he'd been dreading for hours. Another in a futile string of them, he supposed, as he dialed his banker to see if his latest loan application had been approved. There really wasn't any hope in it. He'd gone down this road before, and was getting pretty good at putting on the unemotional response when he was rejected, when what he really wanted to do was punch a hole in the wall. Three holes, as this was his third application.

Sighing as he tapped in the numbers, he thought about Susan…and it wasn't the corporate executive that came to mind when his guard was down. But the corporate executive and the poor village doctor together, in a way that had nothing to do with medicine? *Who was he kidding?* Their worlds didn't just spin around in different orbits, they collided. Good thing there wasn't going to be any attempt to get together, he decided.

Yet what he'd seen Susan do with 'Eleu…

Susan and 'Eleu emerged from 'Eleu's room thirty minutes later, the young girl looking like a totally different child. While she wasn't smiling, there was a little spark of life in her eyes again. Grant saw that almost immediately. She wasn't exactly the same little girl he'd taken bellyboarding on a few occasions, but she wasn't quite so far away from that little girl now. And of all things, she wasn't objecting to her ride in the wheelchair. To be honest, he'd thought she'd hate it.

"Care to push?" Susan asked him, as she stepped aside. "'Eleu has agreed to a short ride in the garden. On the side of the building away from the ocean. She doesn't want to see the water yet." This time it was Susan's turn to give Grant a knowing nod, except from her it turned into a knowing wink. Which almost knocked him out of his sandals, it was so sexy.

Damn, he didn't need this now. There was too much to lose, and being distracted the way he was on the verge of being could be costly. Straightening his shoulders, fighting for his resolve to return, Grant cleared his throat, then asked, "She told you that much?"

"Actually, she told me even more, but some of it was a secret between us girls."

He glanced away before she could give him another of those winks, even though he wasn't sure that she would. But if she did, he wanted to be prepared. "Then the gardens on the north side it will be. Care to join us?" Polite invitation, but he really didn't want her to come along. Didn't want to be anywhere near her, the way she unhinged him.

Susan shook her head. "I have to go down to room…" 'Eleu

looked up at her, clearly stricken. Then reached out in a panic to grab Susan's hand.

Grant moaned inwardly. First his latest loan application had been turned down. He didn't have any collateral to put up against it, but it had been worth trying. Anything was. Then this…and coming on the heels of what could have happened up at the waterfall. Well, that might have been an inward groan, but he felt like groaning out loud over the prospect of spending even more time with Susan. More time, more opportunities to make a fool of himself. At least they would not be alone. "It looks like you're going for a walk first."

Susan smiled down at 'Eleu. "It does appear that way, doesn't it?"

If he were smart, he'd be the one going off to check on another patient, getting away from Susan. But 'Eleu was his patient, and he did want to observe her for a while, especially now that she'd finally reacted to someone. Rather than walking with the two of them, though, he trailed along some way behind, simply watching the dynamics between them. Susan was relaxed and lighthearted again, laughing… He couldn't see her face, but he didn't imagine there would be any frowns there right now. She'd look happy—the way he'd seen her earlier, while she'd been tending the emergency room patients.

Didn't she realize what made her happy? What was it about her that caused her to believe she didn't deserve any happiness? Because she didn't believe she did. She was dutiful, but to something he simply could not comprehend, and she wasn't happy.

Why did he even care, though? Susan was going to buy the clinic out from under him then run it the Ridgeway way, and he absolutely had to get his mind around that cold, hard fact when he was looking at her with anything other than a sharp business eye. This woman who was attracting him like crazy was also destroying him. "Look, could I interest either of you in a shaved ice?" he asked, not because he wanted one but because he wanted to focus on something other than Susan for a while.

"Passion fruit?" Susan asked, then she looked at 'Eleu. "What flavor would you like?"

The child didn't answer at first, but her little face drew into a frown like she was thinking. "Blueberry?" Grant suggested. "Or grape?"

She shook her head no both times, then very quietly asked, "Cherry?"

Amazing, he thought as he trotted off toward the shaved-ice concession stand half a block away from the clinic. Even though he didn't want to think about Susan, he couldn't help himself. After what she'd already done with 'Eleu, Susan *Ridgeway* Cantwell was simply amazing.

"He's a great doctor, but he's been preoccupied lately," Laka said that evening, as the two women sipped fruit juice on the *lanai* of the guest cottage where Susan was staying to be closer to the clinic.

Like before, Susan had worked all day, then agreed to go on the little emergency department's night shift after taking a short rest. So far she'd spent more hours on the job than she could remember ever working, yet she was looking forward to working even more. It was like she couldn't get enough. The more hours she put in, the more she wanted to work on top of that. She'd become absolutely greedy in her passion for patient care, and she loved it, which was why she hadn't left Kahawaii after her words with Grant yesterday. It would have been easy to walk away then return in a few weeks as the medical director, ready to institute Ridgeway policy. Real medical duty felt so good, though, and she didn't want to give it up until she had to.

"I'm not sure what's bothering Doc Etana," Laka continued, "but I think it involves clinic business. I've heard there might be problems, but he isn't saying anything to any of us, so I don't know for sure."

That did make Susan feel guilty, as she was sure that's what was bothering him. But business was business, and the deal to buy the clinic as part of the private Honolulu hospital had been in the works for months before she'd ever come to Hawaii, months before she'd ever seen Kahawaii clinic, or met Grant.

"He has a lot on his mind," Susan agreed, not revealing to Laka her involvement in the affair. "A lot of responsibilities. He takes it all very seriously." Light words for such a weighty situation because, however it worked out, lives would change. "But I'm sure he'll get it worked out." Just not in the way he wanted, and that bothered Susan. Much more than it should, given the circumstances.

Susan and Laka chatted idly for another few minutes before Laka stood to leave. "If you need anything this evening…" she said, on her way to the door.

What she needed, Laka didn't have. "I'm fine, thank you." It was nice having a friend. She didn't have many. Of course, once it was widely known what Ridgeway was doing and that Susan was a Ridgeway, any hopes of a normal friendship with Laka would end. That's just the way it was in her world, and tonight she wasn't feeling good about that.

Once Laka was gone, Susan glanced at the clock. She still had six hours before she was scheduled back on duty, and she wasn't sleepy. She didn't want to go to bed. It was early yet, and she'd taken her dinner at the clinic a while ago, so there was really nothing left to do but sit around and let all the problems surrounding her flood her mind. And there was so much on her mind this evening, so many confused thoughts about the changes happening in her life. So many notions rumbling around in her head that weren't making much sense.

Suddenly, she wanted to walk. A nice, brisk walk might help relieve the stress, which would help her sleep before she returned to duty. So, rather than sitting around bemoaning and fretting her problems, Susan headed out to the beach, promising herself she wouldn't get out of sight of the clinic lights. With a towel slung over her arm, in case she wanted to sit down and watch the nighttime ocean for a little while, she hurried along the well-traveled path toward the sandy patch she'd been able to see from her clinic window. It wasn't the spot she'd found for herself when she'd watched her surfer Adonis, the place where Ryan Harris had died. That was farther up in an area not as secluded as this. She couldn't go back there yet, like 'Eleu, who didn't want to see the beach or the ocean either. Truly, she understood what the child was feeling. 'Eleu wasn't ready to face her fears, and she shouldn't have to.

But 'Eleu was a child. Susan wasn't, which made running away from her fears seem so…pathetic.

But she was pathetic after all, in so many ways. Definitely not *kekoa*.

Continuing on toward the beach, Susan passed a few stragglers on the path. Her mind was still on 'Eleu, and what to do about her. The child had suffered so much loss, yet she was *kekoa*. *Kekoa*, yet so afraid. She needed reassurance. Something tangible to hold on to. Healing in the physical sense was one thing, but 'Eleu needed more. Tomorrow, Susan decided, would be a perfect time to ask Dr Chen about taking 'Eleu to Honolulu, to visit her grandfather. Maybe that's what she needed so she'd feel safe again…reassurance that he was still alive, reassurance on her own that didn't rely on the words of strangers and friends. Maybe she would even volunteer to take 'Eleu to the hospital herself, if Chen permitted it.

Essentially, a house call? Was she actually buying into the idea that a house call was a good idea? Especially after she and Grant had just argued the merits of that very same thing?

Well, just this once it was justified. Twice, counting the call on Moana. Nothing at all hypocritical in that, she decided. Or was there?

Continuing along in the sand, near the water's edge for a few minutes, Susan pondered the dilemma of espousing one thing and practicing another. Condemning house calls, then going on one. Well, wouldn't Grant just have a few words to say about that? And wouldn't he have words to say about the way she was wasting time wandering along the beach, glad to do it, after she'd been so adamantly opposed to wasting time?

This was becoming a dangerous precedent, expressing her beliefs about the way she wanted something done, then doing it Grant's way anyway. It scared her.

Grant's power over her scared her even more. She was taking leave of her usually good, steady senses because of him. Of course, that might only be the romantic lure of paradise and the biological urges working against her. Plus the fact that he was such an extraordinarily good-looking man who practically oozed charm from every last pore. Making all her reactions to him just natural responses. Maybe she should hang out a sign: "Warning! Natural *urges* at play."

Still, there was something else. Something she couldn't put into words or even form a cohesive thought about, for that matter. Because what was going on was so far removed from the bounds of her normal life she wasn't even sure she wanted to explore it.

Which was why she picked up her pace, now intent on forcing her thoughts to something else. Because if she didn't…

As she was trotting along the water's edge, absorbed in looking for shells in the dark, even though she couldn't see them, a solitary form just ahead of her caught her attention. Even without making out the features of him, she recognized Grant, knew his silhouette, felt the sensation he caused in her as goose bumps danced up her arms.

Such an imposing figure of a man, and not just in a physical sense. He had this aura about him. Tranquility, strength. Not like all the other men in her world who fought their way to the top any way they had to. More than anyone she'd ever known, including her own father, Grant was steadfast in what he was about. He didn't waver. She envied that, because that same quest had been going on so long for her and she'd yet to find the answer.

Susan decided not to disturb Grant, but before she could turn back to the trail leading to her guest cottage, he waved to her, and she instinctively went to him. No second thoughts, no resistance.

"Beautiful night," she said nervously as she approached him, and the prickly sensation up and down her arms doubled. He was certainly a problem for her to solve.

"I'm sorry about the things I've said about Ridgeway. I never meant to insult you, but I've been…angry."

It was a sincere apology, and it couldn't have been easy for him. "For what it's worth, I do understand how you're feeling. And some of what you said is warranted." Much of it, actually. She *did* think like a corporate entity first, and her instincts were always to protect the corporate line.

"It's personal, Susan. Which isn't an excuse for what I've been putting you through. But what you could do…" He huffed out an exasperated breath. "It could, and probably will, ruin everything… Dr Kahawaii's dream. Mine."

"Grant, I don't want to ruin the clinic like you think I do. Or your life. That's not my intention. It's never my intention when we take over a medical facility, but the reality is, some things do change. They have to. Though maybe you'll be glad to know that I'm really in conflict over this, too. I like Kahawaii, like the way it operates now, and if I were the only one involved in this decision, I wouldn't make the drastic changes you expect. But I'm not, even with the name Ridgeway. I'm just one of many people involved, pretty much junior of all the executives, and my name doesn't hold as much weight as one might think. It will someday, but not for a long, long time because I haven't been there long enough to earn that status. I'm…sorry."

"Have you ever thought about going back into medical practice? Because you're good. Patients love you, and I think you love working with patients."

That fact was becoming acutely more painful. Honestly, Grant was right. "When I went to medical school, it was never with the intention of being a practicing physician. My father, and his father, who was actually the one who started Ridgeway Medical, believe that the best medical administrators are doctors who have had *all* the training. I happen to agree with that, which is why I went to medical school. But I never intended to do anything other than what I do. I was raised to accept that responsibility, Grant. You have your heritage here, and that's my heritage. And I can hang on to my married name and pretend that makes a difference, but at the end of the day I'm still Susan Ridgeway, the medical director of Ridgeway Medical. It's part of me, just like your sandals are a part of you."

"But you'll take away those sandals, Susan."

"Which is why I'm unsure about so many things now. I

don't want to take away those sandals." That was a huge admission, but it was one he needed to hear. She didn't want him to believe she was the heartless corporate executive who made arbitrary changes only because she wanted to. It was important that he didn't believe that.

"But it's not that easy, is it?" He reached out and brushed his thumb over the frown line on her forehead.

"It should be, but it's not." She drew in a breath filled with melancholy. "I have my obligations and I can't turn my back on them." Even though she might want to. "And what I do does hurt people, I know that. It's hurting you. But in the end we both want the same thing, Grant. We want to provide good patient care."

"You could have done that as a pediatrician, Kekoa. Having your own private practice where you could spend the day doing what you did with 'Eleu. Do you even know you have that in you?"

She laughed at that one. "Me? Working with children? Not a chance! I don't know the first thing about them except for the obvious things a doctor should know. And they frighten me."

"Maybe they frighten you, but you're a natural. You'd be a great mother, too, if your corporate world ever allows you the time. Has anybody ever told you that?"

His words caused her to sputter, because Robert, her ex, had always said she'd be horrible as a mother. In the early days of their marriage, he'd even made the decision *for them* that there would be no offspring in their marriage, suggesting that one of them have a procedure…vasectomy, tubal ligation…to make sure there were no accidents. She hadn't argued, neither had she submitted to a surgical procedure, but she'd always wondered what had caused him to think she'd be so bad, especially as he'd never seen her interact with any children. Maybe it had been *his* wishful thinking, trying to maintain the two-professional status of their relationship. Not that she believed, for a minute, that two professionals in a marriage were incapable of being good parents. But maybe Robert hadn't believed that. Something from his past, perhaps? Whatever the case, that was all behind her now. "Having children? N-not me. What you saw today with 'Eleu is all I have. Fix a little hair, buy a nice dress, treat her the way I would want to be treated under the circumstances. That's the extent of my talent."

"So you've never thought about having any children of your own?"

She had. With her biological clock ticking away, she'd thought about it many times, even as a single mother. But she'd never made a solid commitment to having a child because there was always a longing in her to do it the traditional way. She wanted a father for her baby. A *real* father. Not having a mother herself growing up was the reason she felt it so important for a child to have two parents. Her corporate duties were also part of the consideration because how could she work the hours she did and find time, as a single parent, for a child? She, better than most, knew what it felt like to be passed over for work obligations. "I don't need children. I have corporate employees. That's enough." To her own ears that sounded so trite, but admitting anything else would be giving in to a dream that probably wouldn't come true.

Grant took her beach towel and spread it out above the high-water line, then sat and invited her to sit beside him. "It's a good thing your parents didn't feel that way," he said, as she settled down next to him, taking care not to actually touch him, he to one side of the oversized towel, she to the other, all proper and respectable. The only way she would have it.

"Actually, I believe my father does feel that way. He had his progeny, then quit. And I don't know anything about my mother. So what about you? Any brothers or sisters?"

"Just me. I was enough for my mother to take care of. That's what she always said, anyway."

Susan laughed. "That's right. You were a bad child, weren't you?"

"Well, maybe not downright bad so much as…I suppose the more flattering word would be carefree."

"And the less flattering word would be?"

"Wild. My mother worked all the time. She was a maid at one of the hotels, took in laundry in her spare time. Did some seasonal work on one of the pineapple plantations. She wasn't always around to keep after me, and I took full advantage of that." He laughed. "A lot of the parents kept their children away from me, afraid they'd turn out to be like Mrs Makela's son."

"Well, from what I see, Mrs Makela's son turned out pretty well. So, does she live around here, too?"

"She died during my third year in medical school," he said quietly.

"Oh, Grant! I'm so sorry." She leaned over and laid a comforting hand on his forearm. "I didn't know, or I wouldn't have—"

"No, it's fine," he interrupted. "She was an amazing woman who deserves to be talked about. It's just that most people don't. I think they believe it's out of respect."

"Or maybe people don't know what to say. Like, with me, I never knew my mother. She died when I was young, and my father never spoke of her after that. I don't think *he* knew what to say. And people are so awkward about it, aren't they? But it's not for my sake because, for me, *motherhood* is a strange concept."

"Like *fatherhood* is a strange concept for me. I didn't have a father. Or, let's just say, I did, but he didn't stay around long enough to know whether his wife gave him a son or daughter. The harsh realities of life came crashing down when he realized that being married brought with it responsibilities."

"Then we have something in common," she said. "Both of us raised by extraordinary single parents." Extraordinary in different ways, though. She imagined Grant's mother to be nurturing. Everything a parent should be, which was why Grant was the man he was. A little nurturing would have been nice for her. But in her father's defense, he hadn't run away from the responsibilities when he'd found himself alone with a young child. He'd carried them out the only way he'd known how to. "So, was your mother the one who inspired you to go to medical school?"

"Dr Kahawaii kept me out of trouble by giving me little jobs to do around the clinic, and that was the biggest factor in my decision. I found I loved working at the clinic, even when I was a boy. But my mother supported my choice. I think if I'd chosen a life working on a pineapple plantation she'd have supported that, too. What I did didn't matter so much as if I was happy in my choice. That's what she wanted for me, and she worked damned hard to make sure I got what I wanted."

"Is that why you came home to practice medicine…to honor her?"

"To honor her," he said. "Although I'll admit I was tempted to find a job on the mainland somewhere. I had a few good offers after I finished my family practice residency. Nothing I considered seriously, though." He stopped, sucked in a sharp breath. "Home was…home. You know, where the heart is." The conversation ended there when Grant jumped up and headed off down the beach. Twenty paces away, he turned back. "I'll be in late tomorrow morning. Got something important to do before I start work." With that, he ambled off, leaving her sitting there on the towel, alone, watching him until he disappeared from her view.

Odd man. Interesting man. And, God help her, she was pretty sure she was falling in love with him.

# CHAPTER EIGHT

"ALL I need is six more months," Grant said, although he didn't sound convincing about it. The truth was, there was no place for him to get the money to buy the clinic, and without the money he was going to lose it. No loans, no grants, no nothing. It was as inevitable as it was official. He was out of luck and out of time.

"Then what?" Mrs Kahawaii asked. "Can you guarantee me you'll have the full amount? Or even a fair percentage of the price?" She wrung her hands nervously, glancing down at the floor. Leila Kahawaii wasn't a woman who wanted to make this decision as much as she was one who had to. Grant understood that, and sympathized with her. She was a sweet lady who didn't have many choices.

"No guarantee," he said honestly. "We don't make a profit—in fact, we barely scrape by—so nobody wants to fund a proposition like that, even though everyone I've approached sympathizes with us. I've tried every source I can think of, and have been turned down by all of them. But for the sake of the clinic I have to ask for an extension." And for the sake of her husband's memory, but he wouldn't add that weight to her already heavy burden. That would be intentionally cruel, and he wouldn't do that to her.

"You do know that if I thought you'd be able to honor the agreement I'd prefer selling the clinic to you, Etana. It was my husband's wish, as you know. But I've spent a lifetime sacrificing, and never regretting it, so my husband could have everything he needed for his clinic, and now that he's gone I want to make some changes in my life. He left me with very little except the clinic, and I can't make those changes without selling it." She sighed sadly. "I know you have the vision for what he wanted, and you've stayed true to that, but I don't know what else to do. You can buy Kahawaii now, or I'll be forced to sell it to someone else. And, as you know, I do have a good offer."

Yes, he knew. And, no, he didn't blame her for what she was about to do. She'd been very patient these past six months, waiting for him to put some kind of a deal together. Unfortunately, there weren't many deals to be had for a clinic that operated a quarter of a century behind the times and owned very few assets other than its outdated medical equipment and a nice piece of land.

"Things are going to change," he said, trying not to sound too sad or angry, as he didn't want to make Mrs Kahawaii feel any worse she already did about this deal. "It's inevitable." Her husband's dream, which had become his dream, was about to disappear, and there wasn't a damned thing he could do about it, thanks to Alana. That's where all his anger was directed…at Alana. And at himself, for not noticing what she'd been doing.

Oddly, that anger wasn't directed at Susan. She had a job to do and, while he didn't like that job, he didn't hold it against Susan. At least, not much.

"But your job will be guaranteed. I've spoken with my attorney, and if I accept any offer, that's to be included as part of the conditions. You're to remain on staff. I'd like to dictate that it would be as chief of staff, but I've been advised that anyone purchasing the clinic will likely wish to bring some of their own people into the clinic, so I can't do that for you. If you'd like, though, I can negotiate a much better salary than what you receive at Kahawaii, because I do know that's not nearly what you're worth."

It was a genuine offer. But money wasn't the reason he'd stayed working there. Hell, money wasn't even a consideration, he'd earned so little of it. The funny thing was, when he'd gotten out of medical school, the monthly salary for some of the jobs he'd been offered had been more than he earned at Kahawaii in a year. It didn't matter. He'd never been tempted by the lure of the big buck, as he had everything he wanted, and it felt so good to live by an ideal. Most people weren't that lucky.

Unfortunately, he wasn't going to be that lucky much longer. "I appreciate you looking out for me, but I'm not sure what I want to do at this point."

"I'm so sorry, Etana. I know my husband wanted you to have the clinic, and that's still my wish. If I didn't need the money, I'd be happy to wait, to give you all the time you need to come up with it. Waiting, though, and hoping you can produce something could ruin the deal that's already in the works. And in the end, if you don't come through, that would leave me with nothing. Which isn't the way I wanted to do this, but I don't have any other choices. I can't operate the clinic, even from a business point of view, I'm not a doctor so I have no medical interest in it and, to be honest, I really don't wish to have that kind of responsibility in my life now. My husband lived for his work at that clinic and I honor his memory, but honor won't help me afford to move to Maui to be closer to my daughter and grandchildren, which is what I want to do."

In other words, this was it. End of the line. Kahawaii, as he'd known and loved it, was over. "I understand," he said, fighting back the emotion—the anger, the frustration. "And, please, don't take this the wrong way, but don't include my job as part of your deal. At this point, I'm not sure what I'm going to do, and I don't want to be tied into a contract, especially with the changes I think they're going to make when they take over." He couldn't help but think back to some of Susan's amazement over what was allowed at Kahawaii—the lack of uniforms, the system of charity they extended whenever it was needed. She would change those things and he wasn't sure he had the heart to stay there and witness those changes. "Will it keep the Kahawaii name?" he asked.

"They always use the name Ridgeway in some form," she said, "but I'll ask. It would be nice of them to keep my husband's name on his clinic, wouldn't it?"

Except it wouldn't be her husband's clinic. Neither would it be his. "Yes, it would," he agreed, although he didn't think there was a chance in hell it would happen. Big medicine, like Ridgeway Medical, had its own agenda, and honoring the founder of a small village clinic wasn't even close to anything they cared about.

And Susan, when it got right down to it, was still big medicine.

"Can we get a helicopter?" Susan asked Laka, as she took another look. Kuli Aolani was *hapai,* and not in a little way. She was nine months along in her pregnancy, ready to give birth, and she'd simply wandered in about twenty minutes ago, expecting to do just that. Here. Now. Her labor pains were coming between one and two minutes apart, lasting sixty to ninety seconds, and if what Susan had learned in medical school was coming back to her the way it should, Kuli was way under-dilated for this stage of her labor. Three centimeters and hard labor weren't compatible. Especially as Kuli was feeling the urge to push, even though nothing about her body was ready to let that baby out. "I don't think there's enough time," Laka said, studying the fetal monitor. "Heart rate's getting a little slow. Not critical yet, but right at one-twenty now."

The very lowest end of the normal spectrum. That, in itself, wasn't bad, but the fact that the rate was continually spiraling downward was. "I can't perform a Caesarean section," Susan whispered, sitting back down on the stool at the end of the exam table to have another look at Kuli, hoping a miracle had happened in the last two minutes and she'd dilated some more. But she hadn't. So Susan stood up, did an abdomen probe, only to discover that the baby was trying to move into position. Not good. "When did you say Grant would be back?" she asked.

"He didn't say."

"And Dr Chen left?"

"Went back to Honolulu two hours ago," Laka said, taking another look at the fetal monitor. "It's dropped to one-ten. Look, Susan, I'll call for a helicopter, but I don't think we have enough time for it to get here, and while I've got midwifery skills, that's only for a regular birth. Not this."

Neither did Susan have the skills for this. But Kuli was on the verge of fetal distress now, and it was progressing rapidly. Which left only one option. One she didn't like at all, but about which she had no choice. "Can you handle an epidural?" she asked Laka, hoping she would, as administering the anesthesia wasn't usually considered a nursing duty.

Laka nodded. "I've done it for Doc Etana."

"No pain medicine," Kuli interjected. "I do not want pain medicine."

"It's cultural," Laka explained. "By tradition, Polynesian women believe they shouldn't express pain verbally during childbirth, that the pain is something that must be endured, part of the honor of being a woman. So, because of that, many of the more traditional women will refuse pain medication of any kind."

"Not during a Caesarean section she won't," Susan said, taking hold of Kuli's hand, preparing to explain the situation to the young woman. This was her first child, she was barely eighteen, her young husband was wearing a groove in the tile floor in the hall outside, and Susan desperately wished she didn't have to be the one to perform this delivery, but there was no one else. It did flash though her mind that if this had been a Ridgeway clinic there would have been more than one doctor on duty. Yet those things couldn't always be controlled, could they? Not even in a Ridgeway clinic. Other emergencies happened, other events got in the way. Funny how she'd never thought like this before. It was such a simple concept, which she'd overlooked until now—sometimes real life outweighed procedures and policy, and Susan Cantwell, the doctor, was just coming to realize that. "Look, Kuli. Your baby is struggling to come out. It's fighting to get here, but your body isn't ready."

"Then my baby will wait until I'm ready," Kuli said confidently.

"Your baby can't wait," Susan said. "Did Doc Etana ever tell you if it was a boy or a girl?"

"He said it's a boy, because my baby kicked so hard."

"And do you and your husband have a name selected?"

"We like Ali'ikai. It means king of the sea."

"It's a beautiful name," Susan said, as Kuli's squeeze on her hand intensified. Another contraction, and Kuli barely flinched as its grip hit her. But her hold on Susan's hand told the story, especially as the pain lasted well over the one-minute point. "I have to give you pain medicine, Kuli. Your son, Ali'ikai, cannot be born in the normal way, and the longer we wait, the more danger we're putting him in." She seemed so young that Susan wasn't sure how much the girl knew about childbirth. "Do you know what a Caesarean section is?"

The girl nodded.

"That's what I have to do, and in the next couple of minutes." She'd done it a few times during her internship, when she'd rotated through obstetrics. It wasn't difficult, but it had been such a long time.

"We can't wait?"

"It could harm your baby if we do. So, to do a C-section, I have to give you pain medicine. Do you understand? This is to take care of your little boy."

Kuli was loath to agree, but she did as another contraction started. "I trust you, Doc Susan." Words that should have been comforting scared Susan all the more.

It was time. The fetal monitor indicated that the baby's heart rate was dipping close to one hundred beats per minute now. Distress was imminent, and there was no time to wait. She gave the nod to Laka, who was already setting up the tray to administer the epidural anesthesia. "You'll feel some pressure during the delivery," Susan said, "but no pain. And you'll be awake when Ali'ikai is born."

"Thank you," Kuli panted.

Susan gestured for two of the other nurses to come in, one who would attend to Kuli during the delivery and one who would attend to the baby. Then she ran out to explain what was going on to Kuli's husband, Keoki, and scrub up. But she took only a minute, as the fetal alarm was loud and shrill. Time was up. She had to do this right now!

"Now," she said, coming back into the surgery, looking far more calm and in control than she was, "let's get this baby born." She took her place at the side of the bed. "Is she prepped?"

"Prepped," Laka said. "And anesthesia is running."

"Do you have an antacid going in?" Susan asked, as she began to assess Kuli's belly for the incision.

"Yes, Doctor."

*Doctor.* Nobody at Ridgeway called her that and it sounded so strange now, especially under these circumstances. If any of them knew how nervous she was about this, and how totally inexperienced she was, they would be calling her Mrs Cantwell, the way her employees did. Not Doctor.

"Oxygen?"

"Running fine, Doctor."

Susan decided that a vertical cut was best, under the circumstances. Obstetricians usually did the horizontal line, but time was running out, and she didn't have the luxury of trying to make it pretty, or invisible, the way a horizontal incision would do. So, after one of the assistant nurses rubbed Kuli down with an antiseptic, Susan drew in a deep, steadying breath, picked up a scalpel, and made the midline slice. After which she pushed aside Kuli's vital organs and made an even larger cut in the uterus. "You're doing fine," she said to Kuli, who was, true to her tradition, very quiet. "Another two minutes and you'll be a mother."

Another swift slice and Susan broke the bag of waters, then began to disengage the baby from Kuli's pelvis. "He's a big one," she said as she lifted the baby out with her hands. Then underneath her mask she bit her lip so hard it bled. The baby was not breathing. She gave a frantic look at Laka, who'd only right then noticed the lack of crying.

"How big?" Kuli asked.

In the first thirty seconds of Ali'ikai's life, Susan wrapped a blanket around the neonate, cleared his airway with a bulb syringe, and attempted to stimulate breathing by a little tweak to the baby's foot and one to his chest. But he didn't stir, so in the next thirty seconds she took the ventilation mask attached to the breathing bag one of the assistants gave to her, placed it over his face and attempted ventilation, at the same time watching to make sure his chest was rising and falling. It was, which was a relief because that meant there was no airway obstruction.

Still, the baby did not respond. "Epi," Susan said, handing off the bag to the assistant and beginning chest compressions just after Laka inserted an IV. She'd never tried to resuscitate an infant before, let alone a neonate, and images of her last resuscitation attempt with Ryan Harris came back to her as her fingers pushed up and down on the frail little chest.

No response in the next thirty seconds, however, and in the very short time she had, the potential to save this baby was slipping away. "I want point zero one milligrams of epinephrine to start with," she said, now gaining confidence that her medical school knowledge was still intact. "Push it in fast. And can we get some EKG leads on Ali'ikai?" she asked the assistant who'd been attending Kuli.

"Is there something wrong with my baby?" Kuli cried out, finally breaking tradition. She tried to sit up, but Laka gently pushed her back down and told her to be still.

Susan stopped CPR for a moment, and felt for a pulse in the baby. Her hands were shaking so hard, though, it was difficult to feel anything except her own trembling. So she started the chest compressions again and, with her free hand—chest compressions for neonates took only one hand—she yanked her stethoscope into her ears then placed it on the baby's chest and quit pressing his chest. "Get ready to push more epi," she said. "Up it by a hundredth." Then she listened...held up her hand to silence all the noise in the room, and listened again.

There it was. A heartbeat beginning. Starting slowly, gaining speed. Ali'ikai coming to life. "Clamp his cord," she said, as the surgery doors slammed open and she heard heavy footsteps coming up directly behind her.

"I'll be glad to do that," Grant said. "And close Kuli for you, if you'd like to go tend to the baby."

"Ali'ikai," Susan corrected, as one of the assistants cleaned up the little boy. "His name is Ali'ikai." She bent down to Kuli, who was too frightened to speak, and whispered into her ear, "And he's beautiful. The most beautiful baby I've ever seen in my life." And he was.

"Really?" Kuli asked, through her tears.

"Really," Susan assured her. "But I think he's going to be stubborn, judging from the way he came into the world. Stubborn and loving lots of attention."

The assistant handed the baby, who was now breathing on his own, to Susan, who briefly put him into Kuli's arms. "He's doing fine now, but I need to go get him into an oxygen-enriched atmosphere," she said. "And I'd like to send him down to Honolulu for a couple of days so the doctors there can make sure he's perfect. But hold him for a minute. Get to know your son. Just be careful of his IV line."

"Will he know I'm his mother?" Kuli asked. Her face was bright with adoration as she took her new son into her arms.

Susan watched the baby boy nuzzle into his mother. It was amazing. Five minutes ago the child had been dying…even dead by some definitions…and now here he was, clinging to his mother like nothing had happened. She envied Kuli that. And at that moment, for the first time in her life, she *truly* wondered what it would be like to have a baby of her own. A baby who needed her the way Ali'ikai needed Kuli. A child to love the way Kuli loved her child. Grant had said she'd be a good mother, and now she wondered. For a moment she even saw herself cuddling a newborn to her breast…Grant's son. Quickly she shook away *that* image. "He knows you're his mother," Susan replied, a little shaken by her own vision. "He really does know you're his mother."

"They're so young," Grant said, dropping down onto the chair next to Susan. "Kuli and Keoki. Add their ages together and they equal mine. Talk about feeling old."

She'd been sitting there, numb, for the past hour and a half while Grant had finished taking care of Kuli and making arrangements to transport both mother and son to the hospital in Honolulu. Amazingly, the baby was stable now. He was kicking and crying, and being rather rambunctious for one so new to the world. It was like his difficult birth had merely been a test for his mother, and once she'd passed it he was on to his real life. Mom was doing fine, too, the trauma of a difficult delivery already forgotten.

"When I was that age, the last thing on my mind was marriage, and here they are, not only married but with a baby," Susan said wearily. She was sitting in a chair in the doctors' lounge, her feet up on the chair across from her, and she was smiling in spite of the fact that she was exhausted, both physically and emotionally. What a day's work! She'd not only delivered a baby but it had been a risky delivery. To be honest, she was proud of herself. If anybody had asked her if she could do what she'd just done, she would have told them she couldn't. Emphatically not. When she'd had to, though, when there had been no other choice but her… She pushed the thoughts of what might have happened out of her head because this moment felt good and she wanted to linger in it a little longer. "It's kind of amazing, isn't it, the way people have such different priorities? Kuli told me all she'd ever wanted was to be a mother, and I'm betting that even after her difficult birth, she'll have more children." She sighed. "Do you realize, Grant, that I just delivered a baby?"

"Your first?"

She nodded. "I worked in obstetrics a while when I was an intern, but as obstetrics wasn't going to be my specialty, my experience was limited. It was such a…rush, doing the delivery, even if it was a Caesarean. Do you ever get over the feeling that comes from bringing a new life into the world?" A feeling that the corporate Susan Ridgeway Cantwell might never have experienced if not for today.

"I've delivered well over a hundred babies, and I've never gotten over it yet. You did a good job, Susan, and I'm sorry I wasn't here earlier to take over, but Kuli's due date was still three weeks away. If I'd even thought that she would deliver early, I wouldn't have gone off and left the clinic unattended."

"Unattended?" Susan snapped. "Is that what you consider I'm doing here? *Un*-attending the patients?" She dropped her feet to the floor and scooted to the edge of the chair, deciding to leave before they argued again. Now wasn't the time.

"That's not how I meant it," he said. "And I apologize for insulting you, but I've had a very bad day and I wasn't thinking. Hell, let's just call it one of the worst days of my life then let me apologize in advance for anything else I'll say that will be out of line."

The strain on his face was evident. She'd thought it was from walking in on Kuli's delivery so late into the event. But now that didn't seem to be the case. "That bad?"

"That bad, and worse."

He didn't elaborate, and she debated prodding him. It wasn't any of her business, but curiosity got the better of her. "Anything I can do to help you?" she asked.

Grant shook his head. "You win. But I'm not sure if I'll be wearing regular shoes."

Susan waited for more explanation, but he offered none. Instead, he got up and walked out, leaving her there still proud of herself but now deflated by Grant's difficulties. Apparently, his hopes for buying the clinic had just been dashed. She felt bad about that. Even more, she felt no joy in what should have been her victory. In some deep, dark way she'd wanted him to pull off a miracle. But he hadn't, and now she wasn't sure what to do.

She had twenty-three voice mails, according to her cell phone. She'd been watching the numbers stack up these past few days. She had no doubt who they were from, and by now her father would be good and angry. She'd called him in the middle of the night a couple of times, purposely dialing in so he wouldn't answer, and had left messages saying she was fine and not to worry about her. And she'd deliberately not listened to any of his messages as she knew what they were about. But she was beginning to feel a little guilty now. Which was exactly what she hadn't wanted to feel. Old habits died hard, though , and she was so good at doing the guilt trip, where her father was concerned.

Against her better judgment, Susan picked up her cell phone and punched in her father's private number. His phone rang only once before Walter answered. "Where the hell have you been?" he shouted. Good thing she'd anticipated that from him and was holding the phone away from her ear when he came on.

"On holiday, trying to get away from just that," she responded, trying not to sound too contentious. After all, he could actually be worried about her. Not likely, but there was a chance.

"You haven't been returning my phone calls," Walter continued, his voice backing off a bit but not enough to convince anyone that he was in anything but a bad mood.

"Because this is what I expected from you. So why would I want to return them?"

He didn't pause, didn't miss a beat. "Because that's your job. That's why."

"I'm having a lovely time, in case you're interested." She heard a heavy sigh on the other end of the phone line.

"Look, Susan, I know I promised you some time off—"

"I've only been asking for a few days for three years now," she interrupted.

"But why now? Why, when we're looking at a medical group on Oahu for possible acquisition? Couldn't you have waited—?"

"I've been waiting. But it never lets up, and I needed a break. So I took one." In spite of her father's grumpy mood over it, she didn't regret it at all. "And in case you're worried I won't do what I'm supposed to, don't. I'll be there at the meetings you've got scheduled in Honolulu. I've never *not* been there when it's necessary, you know that." Try as she may, she just couldn't get anger into her voice. Was it due to some of that laid-back, Hawaiian-casual mood finally beginning to rub off on her?

"You sound…different," he responded, his voice softening. "Has something happened?"

Would he even care that she'd lost one life and saved another? Somewhere, far in his past, her father had been a doctor, too. But he'd lost all that. At least, the personal side of it. To him, medicine was business, and business was medicine. His goal was always to deliver the best care possible to the patients in one of their hospitals, but that was an impersonal decision. His whole outlook on medicine was impersonal, and she didn't believe he'd care at all about her very personal brush with it. "I'm getting some well-needed rest, catching up on some reading, seeing some beautiful sights."

"Where are you?" he asked.

"In Hawaii. Being a tourist." As well as a real doctor at one of the clinics they were going to buy, but she wasn't going to tell him that.

He paused for a moment—to calm down, she guessed. Finally, he continued, "Would you want to have an advance look at what we're probably going to buy…get an early inspection of their medical facilities? It's a hospital and several of its affiliated clinics and facilities—"

"I know." And she wished she didn't. "It's called Bayside Regional. I've read the prospectus, taken a look at the report on services, looked over the details for the clinics we'll most likely include in the deal. But, no, I don't want to do an early inspection of anything." The truth was, she was enjoying medical life here so much at Kahawaii that she wasn't ready to tangle with what they were going to do with it. Her time here was short now, and she didn't want to give up any of it. "I'll be there when you are, but until then I'm still on holiday." In a manner of speaking.

Her father didn't respond right away—again. Susan guessed that he wasn't quite sure what to say to her. After all, she'd never openly defied him, not like she was doing now. Normally, he'd request whatever he wanted and she'd acquiesce. That was the dynamic of their relationship. Her father knew that, and always took full advantage. So right now he was probably trying to figure out how to handle a daughter who wasn't quite so quick to give in to him.

Admittedly, she liked this new attitude coming over her. Liked feeling bold and on her own. It wasn't that she'd felt mousy or dominated before because, honestly, she'd never felt inadequate or not up to the responsibilities of her job. She wasn't as experienced as some, but she was good at what she did. Even assertive, if the situation called for it. She liked that.

But she didn't *love* her work and even now, merely talking to her father, she felt the contrasts between what she'd been doing these past few days and what she'd been doing these past few years. In business she was good, but not so fulfilled. In medicine, she was more fulfilled than she'd imagined she ever could be. Which did give her a new sense of empowerment— even over her father.

"Susan, do we need to discuss anything?" he finally asked. "I get the impression that there's something you're not telling me."

There were many things she wasn't telling him, but now wasn't the time, and over the phone wasn't appropriate. She wondered, for a moment, what he would say if she told him she'd decided to stay here and practice medicine in one of their clinics…as a doctor. Of course, that wasn't going to happen. Still, how would he react? Would he argue with her? Or support her and be happy that she'd found something she loved? "Nothing important," she conceded. "I've met some nice people here and I'm enjoying my stay. Perhaps, if you go through with the acquisition, we can buy a company condo over here so I can come back from time to time." Popping into Kahawaii every now and then to volunteer her services had tremendous appeal. More than that, popping in so she could visit Grant was what she really wanted, although she doubted he'd want that. Not when the situation changed between them, as it would when Kahawaii came under Ridgeway ownership.

"Find one, sweetheart," Walter said, his voice finally going soft, the way she liked it. "Pick out anything you like, and we'll buy it. To be honest, I've been thinking it would be nice to have a condo someplace like Hawaii, for an occasional holiday."

Susan laughed. "And when do you ever take a holiday?" she teased, glad the stiffness between them was finally lessening. As much as she was often contentious with him, and he with her, she adored her father, both the daddy and business sides. Although she loved the daddy side much more, even though she rarely saw it. "Last time I recall you taking a holiday was a quick trip to Bermuda, and that lasted all of, what? A day and a half?"

"Okay, so I'm a little obsessed," he admitted. "I'd rather be working."

"Look, I'm fine. You don't need to worry about me. I'm ready for the meeting and I promise I'll answer your phone calls."

"I was worried, Susan. I know you're an adult, been married and all that, but it's still my duty as your father to worry, and when you didn't return my calls… Well, I know you can be stubborn. But, still…"

"I'll answer," she said, laughing. "As long as you don't call me five or six times a day."

"Why do I get the feeling that something else is going on with you? Are you…involved? You're not there with a man, are you?"

If only… "No," she said, on a wistful sigh. "I'm not involved, and I'm not here with a man." Although, from her window, she was watching the man with whom she'd like to be involved heading back to his cottage, and he was a magnificent sight to behold, even from a distance. But his shoulders were a bit slumped and his steps weren't as lively as they usually were. All because of who she was.

Suddenly, she wanted to chase off after Grant to offer him the kind of support he'd offered her. But would he accept her? It had to be so hard for him, having her here, having her watching, and participating in him losing everything he wanted. Well, maybe she couldn't make it right for him, but she did want him to know that she was there for him, if he needed her. "Do we ever divide up our properties?" she asked her father.

"I'm not sure what you mean."

"I'm just thinking, what if we were to take over one clinic

that simply wouldn't fit into the way we normally do business? Would we ever make an exception and allow it to stand alone and operate the way it did before we stepped in?"

"It would be too difficult, making exceptions where we find them. We are coming up on one hundred properties now, and even if a quarter of them operated independently, the logistics of directing that would be a nightmare. In an ideal world that would be nice, but in a practical sense we do the best we can for everyone who needs us. So tell me, why are you asking about that? You've never been interested in that aspect before. In fact, you've specifically avoided it, and concentrated *only* on continuity and standards of medical care."

"No reason for asking." She'd known the answer before she'd asked, so it hadn't come as a surprise. But it was a little disheartening. "Just curious."

"Are you interested in taking on more responsibility? Because you know you're welcome to get involved in anything you want."

More responsibility? What she had on her mind was less responsibility. "Look, I think maybe I *will* go out and get involved with a man, now that you've brought it up. Maybe we can talk tomorrow?"

Before her father could protest, Susan said goodbye, then ended the call. The next thing she knew, she was out the door, on her way to chase down a man for no good reason other than the fact that she wanted to. "Grant!" she called, trotting down the path, through the palms and rhododendrons. *Susan, do we need to discuss anything?* her father had asked. *I get the impression that there's something you're not telling me.*

What she wasn't telling him was that she'd fallen in love with a man…and with his lifestyle. And that it could and would in *no way* work out. Yet knowing that wasn't stopping her from chasing him down the path, quite possibly to her own broken heart.

# CHAPTER NINE

HE WAS failing everybody who counted on him—people who trusted that when they needed medical care, he'd be there to give it to them in the way they expected. With the Kahawaii deal on the horizon now, he could still practice medicine, but not in the way he wanted, and that was the dilemma. To stay, or to go. Could he actually work at the clinic the way it would be structured, remembering the way it used to be?

Well, he just didn't know. He loved everything here. Loved the people. Loved the area. Loved the lifestyle. Yet it was limiting, he did admit. There was a vast world of medical opportunities out there and he'd never explored any of them because his goal had always been to come back here. Hell, his friends Caprice Bonaventura and her husband Adrian McCallan extended him an invitation about once a month to come and work at their clinic in Miami. He worked with them through Operation Smiling Faces, and the transition would be easy. He had a great medical relationship with them.

But could he survive in Miami?

That was a question he couldn't answer, and he wasn't much in the mood to think about it. Wasn't much in the mood to think about anything today. Especially the fact that he was falling in love with the woman who would, ultimately, destroy him.

"You look worried," Susan said, stepping up onto his front porch. He was standing in the doorway, not inside, not outside.

He shrugged. "I suppose I have that right, don't I?" Mild understatement. All this worry was about to cause him an ulcer.

"Look, Grant, I don't know what to say other than I'm sorry."

"You and me both," he said, fighting not to snap at her. Right now he wasn't in the mood for companionship. He needed to clear his head, force himself into a better frame of mind before dealing with Susan, because all he was fit for right now was brooding, being downright grumpy, kicking himself for the all the stupid things he'd done that had got him to this point. He'd be back on duty in an hour and until then the only thing he wanted to do was to catch a few waves, work out his frustrations in the pounding surf. Calm himself down before he made any decisions about anything.

"Look, Susan, I'm not in a good spot here. I like you… maybe even more than that. But you've got to understand that you come with a great big conflict I can't get past. You're about to ruin everything I've worked for, and it's taking everything inside me not to hold it against you personally. I'm fighting to keep Susan Ridgeway Cantwell separated from Ridgeway Medical, but it's not easy, and right now I'm just not in the mood to be reminded of all the people I'm failing."

"And I remind you," she said, her voice barely above a whisper.

Damn it, he owed the people here better than what they were about to get. He owed them the kind of medical practice they had here, the kind they wanted. Owed them in deep, personal ways because they'd put him through medical school. After the recklessness of his youth had cost him any collage scholarships he might have had a chance at, and when he and his mother hadn't been able to afford to send him to college, the people here had contributed, worked hard, saved their money for him. Invested themselves in his future. He was a doctor because of so much generosity, and here he was, on the verge of letting down the very people to whom he owed everything. He'd let them down so often when he'd been a kid, with the way he'd behaved, and now…

Well, it's what they'd always expected of him, wasn't it? Oh, he'd convinced them somewhere along the way that he was different, more responsible. But that hadn't turned out to be the case, and he was bitter, embarrassed… "Yes, you remind me."

"Then I'll leave," she said.

"No, that's not going to fix anything." Susan out of his sight wouldn't mean Susan out of his mind. It didn't matter where she went because with the way she'd found her place in his heart she'd be with him. "Look, how about we meet back at the clinic in an hour? We'll work the shift then maybe we can…" What? What could they do that would get him out of this mess? Or solve what was turning into an impossible situation between them? Susan had her world, her obligations, and he had his. They wouldn't come together, and he wasn't foolish enough to believe that anything would change. Damn, he really needed the beach. Needed to get there *right now* and give himself time to sort it out. Time to figure out what to say to her. "An hour, okay?"

Susan nodded. "For what it's worth, I'm sorry about all this."

Smiling, he stroked her cheek with his thumb. "I know you are."

Susan took a couple steps back. "An hour."

Grant watched her walk away, admiring so much about her…so much other than her obvious physical attributes, which had a nice sway to them gliding down the path. Her walking-away attributes did definitely catch his eye even though he honestly didn't want to have *those* kinds of thoughts now. Of all times! But watching Susan… "Damn," he muttered, turning back into his cottage to grab his board. "My life is going to hell and here I am, thinking about the woman who's in the thick of it." Nothing like heaping trouble on top of more trouble.

She hadn't been on this stretch of beach since Ryan Harris had died, hadn't thought she'd ever return to this place, but she needed to do some serious thinking. Time was running out and this seemed to be the place for her to come to terms with her future. This spot of beach called her back, put her in a mellow mood for those few simple days when all she'd had to do had been to read a book and enjoy the sun. She had some serious facts to face, though. Some even more serious decisions to make.

Talking to her father had only served to remind her of all the obligations and responsibilities she had to Ridgeway Medical, something she'd been trying to forget since she'd come to Hawaii. None of that was so easily forgotten, though. Not with the way it involved the man she was falling in love with. And even without that unexpected bump thrown into the mix, the honest truth was she was pretty sure she *couldn't* return to her old life with the same heart she'd had for it before. Here, in Hawaii, she'd found what she truly loved to do, which was why she needed the time to think. The time to figure out who to make happy, who to disappoint, who to let down.

Stretching out her beach towel in the sand, Susan took a look around the sand berm for a little pile of shells, disappointed not to find any there, before she sat down. Amazing how long ago all that seemed now. A lifetime in only a few days in which so much had changed, so many things had happened. She wanted other things for herself…different things now. She craved a feeling of satisfaction she'd never had in all her years in corporate medicine, yet had achieved in that brief instant when she'd delivered Kuli's little boy. It was such an amazing feeling, and one she'd never forget. One she wanted to repeat.

Maybe it was all a selfish desire. After all, Ridgeway Medical helped little boys come into the world every day, hundreds of little boys and girls in all their various hospitals and clinics. Kahawaii Clinic could benefit from that, which was what she had to keep reminding herself of. Ridgeway Medical wasn't the bad guy here. Its prescribed medical ethos was practiced in places that struggled to maintain good medical standards, and lives were saved because of that. People were healed. In a very real way, what Ridgeway provided made amazing differences in untold lives. But she did have to keep in mind that for her, lately, those differences had become detached. In her capacity of overseeing the set-up of the medical protocol, all those differences came only in the stroke of a pen on a piece of paper or in a phone call. The results were satisfying but the process was not. Neither was it personal. Yet when she'd held the newborn, Ali'ikai, in her hands she'd experienced such a yearning.

Such a perplexing, wonderful change in her life.

Kicking off her sandals, wishing she could simply settle in here, read her romance novel and wait for her surfer Adonis, the way she'd done before everything changed, Susan made herself comfortable on her towel, put her big, floppy hat on and settled back to watch all the activity around her. It *was* nice to come back here, as she did have a special fondness for this spot, but it took her several minutes to glance down to the sweep of beach to where the Harris boy had died.

When she finally did, though, it was as if nothing had happened, nothing had changed. Life was going on in the very best way. There was a mother there with three children, making sandcastles, digging deep into the sand with their yellow plastic shovels and filling pink plastic buckets with wet sand, then up-turning them to form bucket-shaped turrets. The younger child—she thought it was a little boy even though he had a longish mop of curly black hair—was testing the water, running right up to the edge of it so the wave would tickle his toes when it rolled in, then running back to his mother when the wave ebbed.

It was such a beautiful, normal day and what she was experiencing was an amazing thing, being able to come to a place like this, even if only for a few minutes, simply to clear her head. Yes, it really could become addictive if she lived here, running down to the beach at odd times when she had nothing else to do. As unimaginable as all this seemed, she could almost picture herself doing just that for the rest of her life, and being very happy about it. With Grant right there with her.

Except, with the way matters stood now, her destiny was to be chained to a desk. No beaches. No waves. No shells. No more babies to deliver, and maybe that was the single most disappointing aspect of her whole restless quandary. She wanted to deliver another baby. And she wanted to do it here, with Grant, who was the real source of her biggest restlessness—the restlessness she was still fighting so hard to ignore because broken hearts weren't easy, and hers would surely break if she allowed her real thoughts about this dilemma to settle in.

Everything she wanted here with him was changing. Because of her. The cozy life, the ideal medical practice…none of that would happen now. Everything was changing and she shared a good part of the blame for that. Yes, she could go to her father, ask him to exclude Kahawaii Clinic from the deal, but what good would that do even if he agreed, which she doubted that he would? Someone else would buy it because

Mrs Kahawaii was eager to sell. When that happened, Grant would still be in the same situation. Maybe even worse, as she knew Ridgeway standards and practices and who knew what another prospective buyer would do? It could be much worse for Grant.

However it worked out, it wouldn't be what Grant wanted. For that matter, not what she wanted either.

Sighing, Susan glanced down to the stretch of the beach where she'd watched her surfer Adonis, not expecting to see him there at this time of the day yet hoping she would. As her gaze came to rest on *his* spot, she drew in a sharp gasp. He was there, poised at the edge of the water, staring off at the waves. Instantly, the hair on the back of her neck prickled, and gooseflesh rose on her arms. What was it about this man that caused her to react this way? Never before in her life had one man caused that reaction in her, but now there were two.

The guy stirred her in ways no one else did, except for Grant, and it was time to go see if her surfer Adonis was really causing her to react that way or if it was something in the pure Hawaiian air. Something she'd get over when she went home to Texas. Get over her surfer, get over Grant and blame it all on the wobbly mood that had settled over her holiday.

Wishful thinking. Her surfer was pure fantasy, but Grant was everything real and substantial she wanted, and that had nothing to do with pure Hawaiian air or being on holiday. It was a fact of her being now. Something embedded deep in her soul.

As she watched, her surfer went out on his board, and she needed a better look, so she got up off her towel and walked a little closer, as he went belly to the board and paddled away from the shore.

Such an amazing sight. A body that took her breath

away…like Grant's…and gave her goose bumps…the way Grant did. Dear lord, everything was about Grant! Even her fantasy man.

She watched him rise to his knees on his board, and saw Grant there instead. Watched him push himself up to standing, finding his balance at that exact same moment the wave caught him, and again the way he moved so gracefully was the way Grant moved. Meaning…she had it bad. She was totally in love. No denying it. No downgrading it to something much less—an infatuation, lust. None of that! She loved Grant.

As the surfer sailed in, riding above the water, his movements so smooth, Susan turned away, ready to go back to her cottage. Being here, seeing everything that reminded her of Grant, was just making it worse. But as she turned, the shivers tickled up her spine so she spun back around and walked closer to the man on the surfboard, who had now almost reached the shore. When his wave brought him so close to the beach that she could make out more than just his form, she gasped. *She'd fallen in love with Grant Makela that very first day on the beach.* From a distance and at first sight. Even her fantasy lover was the man she truly loved.

"Grant!" Her eyes went to his face, then did a quick up and down, head to toes and back again, as he came ashore. "I, um…I didn't mean to disturb you. I was just out… If I'd seen you here, I wouldn't have—"

"I've liked having you watch me, Kekoa," he said, his voice so oddly thick and quiet it made her goose bumps start to crawl again. "All those mornings before the accident… Collecting your seashells…"

"You left them for me, didn't you?"

"How did you know?"

"Shells wash in on the wave, and there was no wave washing

as far up the shore as I was sitting." She laughed. "And I found the little tag in with them, identifying them as a product of China."

He laughed. "You got me. But why did you come back looking for them if you knew what they were?"

"Because someone had left them, I hoped for me, and I imagined it was the man I watched on the surfboard. But why did you do that?"

"Purely for my own enjoyment. You watched me and I liked watching you, and you seemed to get so much enjoyment from something so simple."

"You knew I watched you?" A faint blush touched her cheeks.

"A man knows when a beautiful woman is watching him. Knows it even if she's hidden herself under a hideous hat. I didn't think you'd ever come back to this part of the beach, though."

"I didn't either. But I needed to…" To think about her future. To figure out what she wanted to do and, in all honesty, what she *had* to do. "I just needed to," she said. "And I've enjoyed watching you, too. The way you surf is amazing."

*"Hee nalu,"* he said. "It's the ancient Hawaiian word for surfing. *Ku mai! Ku mai! Ka nalu nui mai Kahiki mai. Alo poi pu! Ku mai ka pohuehue. Hu! Kaikoo loa.*"

"That's lovely," she said. "What does it mean?"

"It's an ancient chant to coax the surf. *Arise, arise, the great waves from Kahiki. The powerful, curling waves. Arise from the chant. Well up, long-raging surf.*"

"I've noticed that you pause and look out over the water before you go into it. That's what you're saying then, isn't it? You're chanting to the surf."

"It's called a *pohuehue,* and it brings me luck. According to tradition, it keeps me safe. Hawaiians have been saying this chant for hundreds of years."

"How long have you been saying it?" she asked.

"All my life, from the first time I took to the waves. I think I was three or four." He grinned. "I would have been out there sooner but my mother was pretty strict with me."

"But three or four years old is awfully young…"

"I sneaked out of the house. Had an old board I found on the beach, so I'd come down here and pretend. Not really get into the water. I'd put the board on the edge of the water and pretend I was surfing. Of course, what I didn't know was that my mother was watching me. She knew exactly where I was going and what I was doing because she always came to watch me." He pointed to the cluster of palms not too far off the beach. "I was five the first time I decided to take the board to the water for real, and she came running out of those palms, yelling at me." He chuckled. "It was disappointing, knowing I hadn't been getting away with anything, but in a way I was relieved because the first time is the most frightening."

"She let you do it?" Susan asked.

"She went out with me. Wouldn't let me do anything but bellyboard, which was fine as I had no idea how to surf. And she stayed with me the entire time, pulled me up when I went under the water, encouraged me to get back on and try it again. I think that's how my passion for it started…knowing that my mother was here to help me when I needed it. Like I said before, I wasn't always the best child, and I would have done something really stupid, like trying a wave before I was ready."

"My father taught me to ride a bike," she said. "But his idea of teaching me was simply putting me on it and letting me figure out how to ride for myself. He's a great advocate of trial and error, so he stood back and watched when I fell down, then he helped me back up and told me to try again."

"How long did it take you to learn?"

She winced, remembering the skinned knees and elbows.

"After about fifteen minutes I was too battered and bloody to hit the ground again, so I didn't any more. Necessity is a good teacher sometimes."

"A good learner, too," he added. "So…" He nudged his board with his toe. "Want to learn?"

Susan didn't even hesitate before she refused. "I'm still not over the bicycle lesson and that was thirty years ago," she said, rubbing her elbow. Then she held it up for him to see the scar there. "And that's not the only one."

He pretended to examine the scar for a moment, at first merely bending a little to take a look. Then he rubbed light fingers over it, tracing its jagged line. It was only about an inch long, and as narrow as a pencil mark, with its color quite blended to the skin around it now. Grant studied it as if it were a life-threatening wound, however, twisting and turning her arm so he could observe from a better angle. And once he'd seen the scar from every which way he kissed it. As simple as that, he gave her scar a gentle kiss that sent shock waves racing up her arm. "Bet your dad didn't do that, did he?" he asked.

"Bet your mom did," she returned, rather breathlessly. Too breathlessly for such a casual little kiss, but the goose bumps chased the shock waves that, if he was looking, he couldn't miss. He couldn't miss the little shiver that chased the goose bumps either.

"On more occasions than I can remember. Look, for just this little while I want us to be Susan and Grant, two people on a beach who don't have a nasty situation to face once they leave here. This place will be neutral for us. Can we manage that, Susan? See what it would be like between us if we didn't have these other issues to deal with?"

"I, um…I think that… Maybe I should… I really shouldn't…"

"Want me to teach you how to bellyboard?" His stare deliberately dropped to her flat belly, and he cocked a wicked eyebrow. "Nice belly to go bellyboarding on."

She didn't just feel seduced, she *was* seduced. Right here in the open, on a public beach, the man had made her go weak in the knees and at the same time melted away all her caution. She was now a heap of jitters who, like the little crab skittering around Grant's surfboard, trying to run away right that moment, was doing it sideways. Another kiss, another gaze full of sex, and her knees would give out completely, then she'd be down in the sand, skittering sideways with that crab.

*What would a real kiss do to me?* she wondered. "So, tell me about bellyboarding," she finally said, gathering up her courage.

"You put your belly to the board and do some paddling."

"Like surfing, only I'm on my stomach?"

"Except you don't go out far, and you don't try to catch the biggest wave. But other than that…"

"But what if I do catch a big wave?" she asked.

"Then I'll catch you."

"And you don't think I'm too old, or that I'll look ridiculous…"

"Maybe in your world, Susan, but in my world you're never too old to do anything you want to do, and, as far as looking ridiculous, look around. You're in Hawaii, we don't know the meaning of the word."

She loved the way he said "Hawaii"…with the "w" sounding like a "v." Ha-vah-ee. The way those syllables rolled off his tongue gave her a chill. But, then, just about everything about Etana Grant Makela did, and the only ridiculous thing happening here would be her *not* bellyboarding with him, or refusing anything else he offered. It was a once-in-a-lifetime offer that excited her, and unfortunately saddened her because it would never happen again. "So I just paddle? Is that how it's done?"

Grant gave her a warm smile. "I know it's tough, Susan, breaking out of your mold, but you'll enjoy this. I promise."

His promise to keep, she thought as she unbuttoned her jacket and dropped it on the sand. And hers to hold on to for ever.

"Let me give you a couple general instructions," Grant said. "The first thing you've got to do is keep in mind that surfing is all about balancing your body on moving water while being knocked about by breaking waves."

"Um…" she said, wondering how such a simple explanation of mechanics could sound so seductive. Thank God they'd made this beach neutral!

"So, keeping that in mind, the way you'll start off is to walk your board out into the water until you're waist-deep. Then you'll lay your body on the board, taking care to keep your weight centered on the middle of it. The natural tendency is to lean back toward the tail of the board as you're climbing on, but that causes the nose to rise and creates resistance when you're trying to get moving, so make sure you keep your chest above the center point of the board."

"Chest above the center point…" she mumbled. "No leaning back toward the tail."

"I think the easiest thing to do would be trial and error, the way you learned to ride your bicycle." With that, he picked up the board, which was longer than she was tall, tucked it under his arm, and nodded for her to follow him into the water. "The first time you try this you'll probably be a bit wobbly," he said, as they got farther and farther away from the shore. Knee-deep, thigh-deep…

"Do I just climb on?" she asked, once he'd placed the board in the water and started to push it forward.

"Something like that. But the key to doing this well is to be still about it. The less movement, the better. And if a wave catches you, and you go off the board, cover the back of your head immediately with your wrists over your ears and your elbows together." He demonstrated the motion on her by picking up her arms, positioning her wrists over her ears and bringing her elbows together. Then he separated her elbows and kissed her. Full on the lips. This time it wasn't gentle, wasn't a tease. And by the time she slid her hands from over her ears and snaked them around his neck, the kiss had turned into everything she expected from him and like nothing she'd ever experienced in her life.

"This time it's because I want to." Grant's voice was a sensual growl against the roaring of the surf behind them. "If you do."

"I want," she whispered against his lips. A sudden commingling of desire and jitters pooled heavily in Susan's stomach. Somehow she'd known this would happen, and she'd wanted it. Another departure for Susan Ridgeway Cantwell, she thought as she melted into the mastery of his kiss.

His hands were on her now. Strong, soft hands skimming their way down her back… Thank heaven her swimsuit was backless. It was a touch that caused the all-too-familiar gooseflesh not just to rise but to riot, a touch that could only be his. Dear God, how she loved the way he touched her, pulled her harder into him, into his bare chest, until there was nothing between their bodies but the thin fabric of her swimsuit.

A soft moan purred in Susan's throat only to be urgently swallowed by his lips and probing tongue. It was like an eddy, a vortex of pure, raw emotion all wrapped into one kiss as he leaned away to kiss her neck, her throat, a trail leading down into the dipping neckline of her suit. The feel of his lips spread wildfire under her skin, over her skin. And she didn't shrink from the obvious signs that her body was responding all too well to his. Or the hard feel of his response to her as he pulled back, stared a moment at her nipples pebbling hard underneath the black, stretchy fabric, then reached out to stroke one.

"Damn," he moaned, dropping his hand to his side. "They have laws in Hawaii about what people can do on a public beach, and what I want to do…" he wiped the sweat off his brow and expelled an agonizing breath "…will get me jail time."

Yearning stung deep in her core, in her heart as she voluntarily stepped back, already missing the sweet mingling of his keen male scent with the salty ocean air. She'd wanted it all, was willing to give it all, and the frustration over unsated desires and longings like she'd never known in her life would have allowed anything, everything. "Rather than jail, shall we do some bellyboarding?" she asked, her voice unbelievably raspy with need.

His glance immediately dropped to her belly, as he reached out his hand to skim across the smoothness of it. "Damn," he muttered again. "I'm not sure I remember how."

Susan laughed, the sound of it hoarse. "Something about water up to my waist and the less movement the better."

"Trust me, less movement is only good for the water. What I'm thinking right now is about a lot more movement." His voice was hoarse, too, as he pushed the board forward until they were waist-deep…her waist, anyway. They had a way to go before they reached waist-deep for him. "So, climb on." He steadied the board for her.

"How?"

"Belly up over the side. Lift yourself. Except for the board moving about in the water, it's very stable. Won't go under."

Susan studied it for a moment, positioned herself at the side then slid on. It was amazingly easy. So was turning until she was lying parallel to the length of the board, nervous that the whole thing would capsize and roll over with her on top. And it wasn't that she was afraid to go under the water, because she wasn't. They were, after all, in only up to her waist. But she didn't want to make an idiot of herself in front of Grant. She was too old to be starting so many new adventures in her life…collecting shells, learning to surf…and she didn't want it to show. The truth was, she wanted to impress him. "Now what?" she ventured, when she was reasonably sure she wouldn't tip off.

"Sit up. I want you to straddle the board with your bottom situated a little below the center point of your board. That will give you a good feel for it, and also it's a good way to control the nose, to make it swing left or right when you want to change your direction."

Carefully, Susan crawled back up into that position, as Grant steadied the board for her. The gentle up and down of the waves was a nice feeling. Of course, she was so near the shore that at this point the waves had all but petered out. But it felt good, being part of such a mighty force. Felt good, too, being part of something Grant had such passion for. "Is this okay?" she asked, finally bracing herself into what she hoped was the proper straddle position.

Grant responded with something that sounded like a cross between a grunt and a moan, and she noticed he was looking anywhere but at her body position. She was rather pleased with the response. Wondered, briefly, if she could repeat the pose later, without the board.

"So?" she asked, reaching out to lay a hand on his shoulder, even though she didn't need steadying. "What's next?"

He cleared his throat heavily. "Pick a wave that hasn't yet broken…one that is staying even all the way across. Here, so close to the shore, that won't be so rough, but I'm going to guide you out a little farther to give you a better ride. As the wave is coming toward you, but before it reaches you, with your knees swing the nose of the board toward the beach, lie down, and as the wave catches you, start paddling. Cup your hands and paddle alternately, like you're swimming."

"And that's it?"

"That's it. Except stay on the board. If you don't, do what I showed you how to do. And if you should go under the water, stay down for a few seconds before you come back up, so you and the board won't collide."

"Do you trust me to do this on your board?" she asked, as he tipped the board toward the waves and began to push her farther out.

"I'd trust you to do it on me if we weren't on the beach," he replied. Before she had a chance to respond to that, or even think about a response, he shouted, "Good one coming in."

Which immediately set her into a panic, trying to remember something that only moments ago had seemed so simple. But her mind wasn't exactly on surfing right now.

"Nose it around," he shouted, from somewhere off to the side of her. "With your knees, nose it toward the shore."

Immediately she responded to his voice, and as she was bringing the board round, he shouted the next instruction. "Get down!"

She went straight onto her belly, and that was the last she heard from Grant as the wave caught her and she began to paddle for her life. Well, not for her life. But it was an exciting ride, skimming along on top of the water, with its raw power carrying her and letting her know throughout the entire ride exactly who was in charge.

It was an exhilarating ride, and breathtaking, but over all too soon, as the wave died out before she reached the shore and the board simply came to a stop. That's when she toppled off it. Went right off the side, and totally forgot everything Grant had told her about the defensive posture to take. But the water wasn't deep, and at the end of a glorious ride she found herself in the rather inglorious position of having to crawl ashore on her hands and knees. Wishing she had her big hat on so nobody could see who she was.

By the time she got out of the water she was surprisingly exhausted, and she plopped face-first into the wet sand, twisting her head to the side so she wouldn't breathe it in.

"One of the first rules of surfing is that when you let your board go, you've got to find it. Loose boards are dangerous out there."

She raised her head, but not much, and all she could see were his feet. Dropping her face back into the sand, she puffed out a weak "Next time," then shut her eyes, trying to concentrate on finding a little strength to get herself up.

As it turned out, she didn't need that strength, because Grant rolled her over and scooped her up into his arms. "Want to go again?" he asked. He was laughing, his eyes twinkling. And even though her face was caked with wet sand, as was the rest of her, and she looked like an unfortunate sea creature that had beached itself to die, all she wanted to do was stay there. For ever.

"Maybe later," she finally managed. "I think I'm a little too out of shape…"

As she uttered her protest, Grant started to walk, but not in the direction of her beach towel, or even toward the path back to the clinic. Rather, he took her back to the water, and when he was in up to his waist, he dropped her in. "You're a little sandy," he said, as she flailed in the water for a moment, then stood up and grabbed hold of him around the waist. "We need to get some of that washed off before we go back to work."

Back to work. Back to all the cutting realities. What a damper to a perfect time spent on the beach. And to think she'd had plans for what would come afterward. Back to his cottage, or hers, out of the swimsuits, carrying on where they hadn't been allowed on the beach... Maybe it was for the best that the moment had ended. She was in love with this man and every second more with him simply made what she had to do harder. She did have to leave. There really wasn't another choice. That was her real life and everything here...it was still a holiday. A fantasy. A short time she'd remember for the rest of her life. "One more kiss?" she asked, pulling herself closer to him, then pressing her head to his chest, so close to him she could hear the steady, strong beat of his heart. Well, maybe it wasn't the smartest thing to do, but her holiday wasn't over yet.

Neither was her fantasy.

# CHAPTER TEN

"SHE'S being a little grumpy today. She misses her grandfather. Wants to go and see him," Laka explained to Susan, as Susan prepared to do a quick exam on 'Eleu. "She's not eating well either."

"You're not?" Susan asked the girl.

Laka wasn't exaggerating when she said the little girl was stubborn, as 'Eleu folded her arms tight across her chest and stared straight ahead, not even acknowledging Susan's or Laka's presence in the room. Yet the expression on her face wasn't stubborn. It was fear, pure and simple. Her world was changing, and even though she was so young, she knew that, understood the consequences in a deep way. Nothing would ever be the same again for the child, and that was something Susan was coming to understand in her own life as well. Nothing would ever be the same for her either. "Want to go outside for a walk?" Susan asked.

'Eleu didn't even bother to shake her head.

"Maybe down to the beach?"

Again, no reaction.

"Over to the concession for a shaved ice?"

Still nothing. So Susan gave Laka a nod in the direction of the door, indicating that she wanted some time alone with

'Eleu. After Laka hurried through charting her nursing notes and scurried away, Susan pulled a chair over next to the bed and sat down. Her first inclination was to reach out and take the little girl's hand, but that wasn't what 'Eleu wanted, and Susan respected her wish. "I want to tell you about something awful that happened," Susan began. Was this the right thing to do? The right story to tell the child? She had so little experience with children that she truly didn't know. But she had a hunch, and sometimes that's what you had to rely on. At least, that's what she was relying on right now.

"It happened one day when I was out at the beach. I'm actually on holiday right now from my real job, and I was by myself, sitting on my towel, reading my book. I like to go to the beach in the morning to collect shells and spend some time doing the things I don't get to do when I'm at home, because there are no beaches where I live."

She paused, and waited for a response, but 'Eleu was still being stubborn about it. So Susan forged on. "One day, I saw a whole lot of people all running toward the water, so I went, too. A young man, a *haole*..." She deliberately mispronounced the word to see if that would catch 'Eleu's attention, and it did. She shifted her gaze to Susan for an instant, before going back to her straight-ahead stare. "He'd been surfing, and he didn't know how. He had an bad accident, hurt himself very seriously." No need going into the grisly details. 'Eleu didn't need that. "By the time I got to him, his friends had him out of the water and were trying to help him. Then I tried to help him. I worked hard for a long time, trying to help him." As the words tumbled out, Susan's hands began to shake. "And I kept trying, but I couldn't do anything. I couldn't..." Her voice broke, and no more words would come.

'Eleu looked over at Susan, and their eyes met. 'Eleu understood...understood far more than a seven-year-old should ever have to. And she reached over to take Susan's hand. "I couldn't help my grandfather," she whispered. "He put me up on the boat, and when he did…"

"It wasn't your fault, 'Eleu."

"But I didn't swim well enough. If I could have gotten up on the boat myself, *kupuna kane* could have gotten out of the water before the shark…"

Susan shook her head. "We can't blame ourselves for the accidents, 'Eleu. Your grandfather wouldn't want you to blame yourself, would he?"

'Eleu thought about that for a moment, then shrugged. "But you blame yourself for the *haole*'s accident, don't you?" She said *"haole"* with an emphasis to let Susan know the proper pronunciation.

"No, I don't blame myself. But I do feel bad about what happened to him, and that's different. What happened to your grandfather was not your fault, and you shouldn't blame yourself. But you can feel bad for him. And you can feel frightened because everything is so mixed up in your life right now. The accident with the shark, though…that was nobody's fault. Not yours. Not your grandfather's."

"Your *haole*. Did he live, or do you feel so bad because he died?"

"He died," Susan replied, her voice barely above a whisper.

"I'm sorry," 'Eleu said.

"So am I. And I'm sorry about your accident, 'Eleu. And about what happened to your grandfather." With those words, the child tumbled into Susan's arms and sobbed until she had no tears left. Susan cried silently with her until all her tears were shed, too.

Grant turned away, as the lump in his throat was about to choke him. Susan was so good with the child it made him wonder why she'd never chosen pediatrics as a specialty. Maybe if she had, she'd still be a doctor. God only knew, there were too few doctors around with the natural ability she had.

It galled him that she wasted so much talent by *not* being a practicing doctor. Galled him to the point he wanted to slam his fist into the wall, which had as much to do with his futile battle against Ridgeway Medical as it did with how Susan wasted her talent by being part of it. Then there was Alana, and his own stupidity… So much anger for so many things.

As Susan stood to leave 'Eleu's room, promising to return in a little while to take the girl for a walk, Grant hurried away. He simply wasn't in the mood…after what could have happened on the beach with Susan, after what he'd seen between her and the girl, after the phone call from Bayside Regional about 'Eleu's grandfather… "Damn," he muttered, balling both fists, even though he really wouldn't do anything so dumb as to break his knuckles on a cement-block wall.

"Grant?"

He pretended to ignore Susan, and picked up his pace.

"Grant?" she called again, her footsteps on the tile floor sounding faster. "We need to talk."

Talk. What good was that going to do when everything around him was going to hell? It wasn't Susan's fault, though. None of it. So, drawing in a deep breath, he stopped, and she caught up with him.

"I thought we were going to talk after we came back from the beach," she said, as he resumed his pace, and she fell into step with him.

"We were, but I haven't had time." He saw the look on her face change from friendly to guarded.

"Well, time or not, I do want to ask about the possibility of taking 'Eleu to see her grandfather. The child misses him, and

I think she'd do much better if she could just have a little time with him. Something to reassure her…" She stopped, and grabbed hold of his arm. "What's wrong?" she said, almost under her breath.

What wasn't wrong? "In my office," he said, taking hold of Susan's arm and hurrying her along until they were behind his closed door. Bad news on bad news. Except for a few nice moments in the water with Susan, he hated this day.

"It's about 'Eleu?" Susan asked.

Still trying to resist saying the words out loud, Grant nodded instead.

"Her grandfather? *Kupuna kane*. He didn't…?"

"No, he didn't die. But he had another stroke this morning. They got a clot buster into him to limit the damage, but since he'd already had one stroke, plus the leg amputation…" He swallowed hard. "He won't be coming home to take care of 'Eleu. The goal is to get him into a long-term nursing facility. Which means…"

"She's an orphan?"

"Unless we can find another relative who wants to take her in, yes, she is, for the second time in her life."

"And what will happen to her in the meantime?"

"I've agreed to keep her here, at the clinic. It's not a real home, but it's better than the alternative."

"A foster home?"

Grant shook his head. "The children's home. There aren't enough foster parents to fill the need for them. So the youngest children go to families and the older children go to an institution."

"No!" Susan gasped. "You can't allow that to happen."

"And I can't take her in myself either. In case you haven't noticed, I don't live the most normal of lives. No one's going to allow me to take in a little girl." He said that not because he didn't want to take care of 'Eleu, because he might have. But his life was so up in the air, and getting worse by the day. Nobody in their right mind would approve his lifestyle.

"Let me go talk to her grandfather. I'll take 'Eleu to see him and maybe he'll give me the name of someone who would want her."

"That's what I was thinking, too, but I don't think he's ready for his granddaughter to see him yet. We can make that assessment when *we* see him."

"We?"

"I need to go, too. Right now, I'm the one who is taking care of 'Eleu and I need to reassure him that she's in good condition. I know you mean well, but he…he trusts me." All the people here trusted him. So maybe that was the final answer after all. Maybe he should simply settle into a medical routine working for a medical employer that would never understand the ways of the people here, and do what he could under the circumstances for those who relied on him. People like 'Eleu's grandfather.

"It means everything to you, doesn't it? The clinic. The way you practice medicine. The people," Susan said a little later as they drove along the coastal road on their way to see Ka Nui.

"I didn't go to medical school with a lot of grand ambitions. All I ever wanted was to come back here and run a medical practice the way it should be." Grant paused, swallowing hard. "They sent me to school, Susan. Every last one of these people here sacrificed beyond their means to get me to where I am today so, yes, all this means everything to me." He shook his head, and didn't say another word until they reached the clinic where 'Eleu's grandfather was.

"Look, before we go in, I want to apologize for the way I've been acting. I've got a lot of problems right now, and I know I'm not too easy to be around. In fact, I've been pretty damned moody. So, in my long list of apologies, let me also add that what happened between us this morning…it shouldn't have. I shouldn't have kissed you, or anything else, because it's just too complicated and, like it or not, only the beach is neutral for us."

"That's it?" she snapped. "Seduce me, tell me it's too complicated, call it a distraction, then apologize and make everything better? That's what I am to you…a way to get your mind off your problems for a few minutes?"

He actually chuckled over her little outburst. "Well, you're right about part of it. You are a distraction. But not in the way you think. I wasn't using you to get my mind off my problems." He reached over and brushed a strand of hair back from her face. "Believe it or not, you're a very sexy lady. You're smart, you're fun to be with, one of the best natural doctors I've ever seen, and the list goes on. And if it were any other way, I'd be doing whatever I could to keep you on my mind and have you distract me, because I'm falling in love with you." He leaned over, unfastened her seat belt, and gave her a very gentle kiss on the lips. "I wish our circumstances were different. You don't know how much I wish that." That said, he unfastened his own seat belt, hopped out of the Jeep and walked around to her side to open her door.

But she didn't get out right away. "What if I changed my circumstances?" she asked. "What if I bought the clinic myself, not as part of Ridgeway Medical?"

Too little, too late. Had he been able to save Kahawaii Clinic, he'd have been down on one knee right now, proposing marriage. But he couldn't. "You can't do that, Susan. And I don't have anything to offer you here anyway. No stability. Not even a future." He held out his hand to help her out, but she refused it. "Look, we both know there are several obvious conclusions here.

I could quit and go back to Texas with you. Or you could buy the clinic, as you offered to, but neither of those would work for us. That's not the kind of people we are. We wouldn't be happy with the kind of compromise we'd have to make and, in time, because of it. we wouldn't be happy with each other."

"Meaning?"

"Meaning it's the same old thing. We're stuck with different lives. I resent what Ridgeway Medical is doing to Kahawaii Clinic and even though I don't hold that against you, in time I'm afraid my feelings might spill over. And they're not going to change, Susan. You can't…*nothing* can change the way I feel, change the things I want." It killed him to say those words, but he had to be honest. Believing the two of them had a future was foolish when he hated such a vital part of her life. He loved her all the more for wanting to buy the clinic for him, but he didn't deserve it. He'd created the mess that got him to this point, and having Susan fix it would only come between them.

"But it's not your fault you haven't earned enough to buy the clinic. You do a wonderful thing here, and you're being penalized for it."

Time for the bitter truth. He hadn't wanted to tell her how he'd come to lose the clinic. Susan was so staunch in her successes and here he was, with his life in such a mess because he'd been so foolish over a woman. Well, wouldn't that just throw out anything good Susan thought about him once she knew?

"I did earn enough," he confessed, "for the down payment Dr Kahawaii had asked for. I'd saved every penny I'd made, and had a little set aside from my mother's inheritance. The deal was set. What you're seeing now isn't a result of anything but my own stupidity."

"I don't understand," she said, clearly confused.

"A woman. I lost everything because of a woman. Her name

was Alana, and I didn't love her, didn't even know her, but for some reason I really can't explain, I got involved with her. Thinking back on it, I don't know what it was about her that I thought I wanted but, whatever it was, she moved in with me, and when I wasn't looking, she took every penny I had. It wasn't much, but it was enough to ruin everything I ever wanted. In the end she said I *owed* it to her because I was always too busy at the clinic and I didn't pay attention to her. She claimed she earned what she took for putting in one lousy year with me. So it's my fault that I lost my chance to buy the clinic. And you know what, if I hadn't been so stupid, you and I might have met on that beach under different circumstances…without Ridgeway Medical coming between us."

"And you're seeing Alana in me. Is that what this is about? To you I'm just another woman who's about to take away your clinic…your dream?"

His dream had changed. Susan was such a huge part of it now. The part he wanted most. "That was never it, Susan. But how can I let you sacrifice anything after what I've done? You don't deserve it, and I don't deserve you."

"Yet you were the one who kissed me, Grant, the one who started something between us."

"And I make bad decisions, as you now know."

"You're calling what we were starting a bad decision? Or are you calling *me* a bad decision?"

"You were the one good decision, Susan." He reached out to stroke her cheek, but she jerked away from him. "The bad decision was everything else I've done. I did what I did and I lost everything I wanted, and…"

Susan drew in a breath. "And I got it. You're right—we can't get past that, can we?"

\* \* \*

Bending over the sink in the ladies' room, Susan splashed cold water on her face, then let it drop back down into the basin as she gripped the edges, not able to stand up yet. How could she have opened herself up the way she had, and allowed herself to hope for something so…impossible? People made mistakes…she had Robert Cantwell as her testament to that. Grant had Alana, and she didn't hold that against him at all. But the outcome…even though he said he didn't blame her, in time she feared he would. How could it not come between them, one woman taking away his means to have his dream, and another buying that dream right out from under him?

It was time to move on. She'd thought about it off and on these past days, when she'd considered the impossibility of the situation, but now it was really time. Maybe her father had been right in refusing her a holiday. Look what had happened!

Straightening up, Susan studied her face in the mirror for a moment, trying to fix a dispassionate expression over the look of a broken heart. She wanted to cry, to scream, to kick over the trash can next to the door. But what good would it do? The wheels of this deal were already turning. Once her father started the deal, nothing stopped him. Nothing or no one had the power or influence, including her. And the deal her father was making was the deal that lost her her dream.

Neither she nor Grant would win in this one. Two people, all their dreams gone.

"Damn," she snarled, yanking a paper towel from the dispenser, dabbing her face with it, then wadding it angrily and lobbing it into the trash. "Damn it all!"

Behind her, two uniformed nurses walked in, cast her wary glances, and scooted around her as fast as they could. Two nurses who would be under her employ shortly, like Grant would. Grant working for her…no! It wasn't right. He wouldn't survive under the rigid standards they demanded. Their style wouldn't suit his. She knew that with all her heart. And as for the people who needed him…

She couldn't help it. On the way out the door she kicked the trash can, then limped a little into the hall, where Grant was leaning against the wall, waiting for her. He opened his mouth to speak, but before he said a word she shoved her palm out to stop him. "Look, there's nothing more to say. It is what it is. I accept that."

"It's not your fault," Grant said. "I understand that."

"I'm glad you do," she said, the anger in her voice giving way to the sadness she was now feeling. "Because I don't. Of all the people in the world I could have fallen in love with, look who I picked. A man with principles that just won't allow me in. Maybe that's what I love the most about you…your ideals." She managed a smile. "And the way you ride the waves. Look, Grant. To make it easier on both of us, I'm not going to return to Kahawaii with you. There's no reason to, so this is what they call a clean break. I'm sorry…" She turned away, but he reached out and grabbed her hand, pulling her back to him.

"I'm sorry, too," he whispered, pulling her close. He held her there for a moment, pressed her tight to his chest, close to his heart. Then he finally let go. "So, is this where I start calling you *Boss?*" He tried to sound light about it, but the misery in his voice came through.

"That's not funny," she said, fighting back tears. Through a hazy mist, she looked up, took one last look at Grant's face, then pulled away from him and headed off, almost running, down the hall. Only a few steps away, though, she stopped dead in her tracks when a group of men emerged from what appeared to be the business office. One of those men was her father. Walter Ridgeway, leading the pack.

Susan spun around quickly to see if Grant was still there, but he was gone. Thank heavens for small miracles. "Father," she said, almost coolly, turning back around to the group.

He took a quick appraisal of the way she was dressed… casual khaki shorts, traditional Hawaiian floral top. Sandals! "Susan," he said, almost as coolly. "I didn't expect to find you here today. Especially not…" He didn't say the words, but he gestured with his right hand to the way she was dressed, and one slight flick of the wrist said it all.

"I'm not here on business," she said, then stopped because, in a sense, she was.

"Then why, exactly, are you here?" he asked stiffly, then leaned forward and said, almost under his breath, "Especially dressed like that?"

"Can we go and find someplace private to talk?" she asked.

"I'm about to take a tour of the facility."

"Five minutes."

He considered her words for a moment, then shook his head. "We'll have dinner later tonight." As he started to walk away, Susan reached out and grabbed his arm.

"Tell me, Father, why what we do is so important. Tell me that it is, that in order to provide the best medicine for the largest number of people we have to turn it into a corporate matter rather than a medical one. I need to hear that, need to know that what we do makes sense."

"Susan!" he whispered, glancing at his business colleagues to see if they were paying attention to the spectacle. "Not now. Please."

"Now," she said adamantly. This was the first time she'd ever gone against her father, the first time she'd ever spoken up for herself. It felt good. Better than she could have ever imagined, because she had a real stake in the argument. She cared about this deal. The other deals made for Ridgeway Medical were merely impersonal acquisitions but this was…Grant's life. And a life she so very much wanted for herself even though it would never be hers. One she was trying to save for the man she loved, even though she would never share it with him. "I want to talk to you *now!*"

Her slashing tone must have done the trick because he stepped away from Susan for a moment, excused himself from the group of men, then took her by the arm and practically dragged her into the office from which he'd come, shutting the door with a bang once they were inside. "What's so damned important that you'd embarrass me in front of my colleagues this way?"

"Your colleagues? Don't you mean *our* colleagues? I have an interest in the company, too."

"So you do," he admitted. Standing rigidly by the door, his face a lifetime full of scowls, his back so straight and starched it looked like it would snap if he bent over. Her father didn't get angry. Impatient, yes. Put off, all the time. Never angry, but he was on the verge of it now. "And I've been wondering about that for a while. Wondering what your intention is with Ridgeway Medical."

"So have I," she admitted honestly. "I guess I didn't realize I'd been so transparent in my…discontent lately."

"I'm your father, Susan. I know your moods."

"I'm glad one of us does."

That caught his attention, because Walter stepped away from the door, then walked across the office to the window, where he leaned against the ledge. "So what's this about?"

"I haven't really wanted to be involved in the pure business of the transactions we make, the medical facilities we purchase. I made it easy for you to exclude me, made it easy for me to exclude myself. And that's worked…for both of us, I think. For me, it's been easier to think of myself as a real doctor when I've been overseeing the continuity of medical care in our facilities. And that's what I want…to be considered a real doctor. I've always wanted that. That's why I've excluded myself from so many things."

"For God's sake, Susan! You're not excluded. Not since I deeded over part of the company to you after you graduated from medical school."

"You did that to keep me from going into a real medical practice, Father. I've always known it was a bribe, because you've always known I loved the pure practice of medicine, patient care. I think you've always known that I was better suited to work as a doctor in one of our clinics or hospitals than I was directing medicine in all the facilities. Which is why you gave me a percentage of the corporation, even though I was so young. You deeded me fifteen percent, gave me a nice title and told me it was my obligation to make sure that the divisions under me ran smoothly because you wanted to keep me in the family business…from your father, to you, to me. I understood that, and accepted it because there are no other Ridgeways who could take over. And you've got a lot from me, because I'm good at what I do."

"Very good," he agreed. "So, what's your complaint, Susan? Because you've got one, haven't you?"

She nodded, taking her place at the door, assuming her own rigid pose there, hoping to God her frown didn't cut as deeply as her father's. "Not a complaint. A request. Not as your daughter, but as a partner you respect."

He cocked an inquisitive eyebrow. "Go on."

"I want you to leave the Kahawaii property as it is currently run."

"That place is an outdated, understaffed insult to good modern medicine. It's situated in a great area for business, the only medical treatment facility for miles, and the numbers we ran on it show that it has a great more potential than it currently realizes. If not in its projected medical output, then in its property value. It's my intention to buy a nice little piece of property nearby, sell the existing clinic to a developer and build an entire new structure with the profits, and have some left over for operation funds. A very nice deal, Susan. We can give those people much better medicine than they've ever had."

"No, we can't. What they get there is the very best personal medicine. It's what they need."

"And they don't have to pay if they can't afford it, which is a poor way to run a business."

"We'll change that, won't we?"

"We won't be heartless about it, and we'll do our best to respect various needs as we always do, but we do have to structure our facilities to be financially responsible, especially if we want to turn this one into a larger, more thriving operation. You know that. So, yes, there will be changes. I mean, I know Mrs Kahawaii employs some local doctor now, and what they take in is laughable…not nearly enough to do what I want us to do. It's an admirable situation, but not practical. So I don't understand where you're going with this."

"What about the staff?" she asked.

"Guaranteed jobs for a year, if they follow the rules."

"And if they don't?"

He shrugged. "You'll fire them. That's part of what you oversee, and you'll do what it takes to get the clinic staffed properly and run efficiently. You said it yourself, you do a good job of it."

"And they'll have to wear real shoes," she said, not so much for her father's benefit but merely as a thought.

"Of course they'll wear real shoes," Walter Ridgeway snapped. "What the hell's wrong with you, Susan?"

"Leave it alone," she said. "Leave the clinic alone. No expansion, no changes. You can buy it, I'll manage it like I do all the others, but I'm not going to change the operations or the personnel. The people in that area need the kind of medicine practiced at Kahawaii, and to take that away from them…" Away from Grant. "It's not right."

"If you don't change the operations here, Susan, I'll hire somebody who will. Any number of people would be glad to come in and take that over for me."

That much was true. It was a good job, if that's the job you wanted to do. But she didn't. Not any more. "Then I'll quit," she said, her voice almost a whisper.

"No, you won't," he snapped. "You've invested too much time, too much energy to walk away from Ridgeway Medical."

That much was also true. But he also meant that she was a product of her father's investment, and he'd invested the time and energy, too.

"And I don't want you to leave, Susan. I know we don't always get along, but I like having you in the company. I know your motives are always in the best interests of the hospitals we buy and run, and I trust that more than you can know. Maybe I can up your percentage, to convince you to stay?"

All that, plus the fact he simply didn't want to train someone else to do what she did. It would take a year, and time was money. She was valuable to her father, not as a daughter but as someone who helped run his corporation.

Susan heaved out a weary sigh. There was a way to win, a way everybody could win. It wasn't the decision she wanted to make, but it was the only one she could, and still do the right thing. Funny how her definition of the right thing had changed these past few days. "I want you to leave the Kahawaii Clinic alone. No arguments, no trying to convince me what a bad business decision that would be. So, how can I get you to do that? What will it take? What kind of business deal can we work out?" she asked, even though she knew what she wanted would come with a high price.

"What I want is that you'll stay on in your position at Ridgeway, do the job as you've always done it. If you'll do that, I'll leave Kahawaii Clinic exactly as it is. In all aspects. Where it is currently located, same staff, no changes. You can do what you want with the clinic so long as you stay with Ridgeway Medical. That's my deal."

The deal she'd expected from him. Everyone won but her. Well, it wasn't like she was selling her soul to the devil. Yet it wasn't the way she wanted this to end either. She wasn't stupid, though. There was no way everyone could get what they wanted. At least Grant had, which was the most important thing. *The only thing.* "Then it's a deal. I'll be staying with Ridgeway, and I suppose you'll be wanting a contract drawn up to make it official." That said, Susan spun around, opened the door and charged into the hall, straight into Grant.

"Susan," her father called, following her out. "I'm your father. I don't want us to be..." He stopped when he saw Susan in the arms of a man.

"Walter," Susan said, pushing herself away from Grant. "This is Dr Etana Grant Makela, director of medicine at Kahawaii Clinic. Grant, this is my father, Walter Ridgeway, owner of Ridgeway Medical." She looked up at Grant, trying to fix a hard expression on her face. After all, it was strictly business now. That's all it was, and this was her first step to prove it. "Congratulations, Dr Makela. We've just had a meeting and decided that after we've taken control of Kahawaii Clinic we will leave it as it is. There will be no changes made."

No changes in the way she was feeling either. She loved Grant with all her heart…a heart that was shattered.

# CHAPTER ELEVEN

"It's been nearly a month, Susan," Walter said from the office doorway. "And you've barely spoken a word to me other than what is necessary for the job. After all this time, don't you think you owe me an explanation? Tell me what I've done?"

She glanced up from the equipment forms she'd been poring over the past hour, giving him only the slightest acknowledgment with her eyes. "I'm busy," she said flatly. "Trying to get caught up."

"You've been busy every hour of every day since you returned from Hawaii, and normally I'd say that kind of dedication to the job was a good thing. But I'm your father, Susan, and I know you well enough to see that something is wrong. I thought you'd eventually tell me what happened to you on your holiday, but I'm getting tired of waiting now."

She could hear it in his voice, that thin-edged patience. He really wasn't patient. In fact, if she could venture a guess, she'd bet he was pretty near his snapping point. But that was fine. Let him snap. Let him explode! She didn't really care. Her father had backed her into a corner and this was what he got for it. A dutiful worker who gave her all to the company, with nothing left over for anyone, including him. It was easier that way. She had less time to think, and other than what was required here she really didn't want to think. "Nothing happened on my holiday that would interest you," she told him. "That's what I've said every time you've asked, and what I'll continue to say. Nothing happened. Nothing at all." Except that she'd fallen in love with a man she couldn't have.

But Grant had got his clinic, and she did have that consolation. She'd made sure nothing had changed for him except he now had better access to supplies and medicine. And nothing would change as long as she stayed in her position. Her father had promised her that much, and she trusted his word as long as he was getting what he wanted from the deal—which was her. So, Grant was set. He didn't own the clinic, as he would have liked, but he had everything else the way he wanted it, and she was glad for him. Glad for the people who relied on him, too.

"But you won't speak to me, Susan. Won't give me a chance to make things right with you."

"And that matters?"

"When have I ever given you cause to think that I didn't care?"

"Oh, I think you've always cared, in your own way. But you've cared more for your business deals than you have for me. I asked for one thing. One simple thing, and you refused. Then you turned my request into a business deal!"

"Is this still about that damned Kahawaii Clinic? Because I did give you what you wanted, Susan. I left it alone. I haven't touched it. I've permitted it to be a drain on our other facilities and suck resources right out of the company without putting anything back in their place."

"Yes, you gave me what I wanted, didn't you? But you attached strings. You couldn't just do it because I asked you to." And at such a high cost.

"I still don't understand your attachment to that place," he said, sounding exasperated now.

She huffed out an impatient sigh, and shook her head. "You know what? I've put in enough hours today." She glanced over as he pushed back the sleeve of his shirt to check precisely how many. Judging from the frown on his face, ten weren't enough. "I think I'm going to go home now. Maybe we can talk in the morning." Maybe, but she doubted it. As she stood, she witnessed something she'd never seen before. Her father was unsure of himself. Ill at ease. Standing there in the doorway, so imposing, the man looked like he wanted to say something but wasn't able to. Odd for someone who was so far past the point of discussion. But she'd never seen uncertainty on him the way it was settling in now. So she waited. Only for a moment, though, before he stepped out of her way and hurried down the hall.

As she punched the elevator button, however, he stepped around the corner and came up behind her, without saying a word. She thought about turning around and simply asking him what he wanted to say, but she wondered if there was really a point. Several seconds later, as the elevator doors opened, and her father had still said nothing to her, she stepped inside, then turned to face him.

"I think you should do it," he said, as the elevator doors shut.

Susan immediately hit the "Open" button, then waited for the doors to part. "What?" she asked, glad to find that he was still standing there.

"Go after that young man, if he's the one you really want."

"What young man?"

"Dr Makela. Didn't you fall in love with him? That's what this is about, isn't it?"

She was too stunned to answer, which was just as well because the elevator doors tried to jerk closed in protest, and the warning alarm began to sound. So Susan let the doors close but immediately hit the "Open" button again. "What makes you think I love him?" she asked, before the doors had opened all the way.

"You've made a big sacrifice for him. Giving up what you wanted so he could have what he wanted... I saw it, didn't want to admit it to myself, but it was there, Susan. And so obvious."

"Obvious, maybe. But you didn't leave me another choice, did you?"

"Maybe I didn't. And maybe I should have listened better. Or been a better father. Stepped aside as your business partner and done it differently."

"What would you have listened better to? Your own ultimatum? Do it your way or you'd find somebody else to replace me? Give me my one request but at the cost of something you knew I didn't want? Well, I heard every word you were saying, and you won. I'm here. Doing the job you want me to do." The doors began to jerk again, and the alarm started once more. This time she decided to let them close, but it was her father who shoved his shoulder in to stop the doors from closing.

"Nobody won, Susan," he said, stepping inside, then gesturing to one of the company employees to step back when she tried to step in, too. "Not you, not me, not that young man who's in love with you. And I realize, more and more every time I look at you, you haven't been happy here for quite a while, have you? You weren't happy long before you went to Hawaii."

It did surprise her that her father had noticed, but she wasn't going to read too much into that. "Not as happy as I would have liked," she said stiffly.

"And what makes you happy, Susan? I want to know because, believe it or not, I do want you to be happy. I may not have ever said that to you in so many words, but it does matter to me."

Again, she was surprised. "What makes me happy is what doesn't make you happy." Honest answer. "I want to practice medicine. Be a doctor who deals with patients. I spent several days doing clinical work at Kahawaii Clinic and I loved it. I told you after I graduated from medical school that I loved it, but you shoved the corporation in my direction and guilted me with my obligations to it. I'm dutiful, I've always done what was expected of me, which shouldn't ever be considered a weakness. But it was. It was a weakness and my downfall."

"You worked as a practicing physician for several days, and you know for sure that's what you want to do?"

"I delivered a baby, Father. Did a Caesarean section and brought a healthy little boy into the world. It was like…like nothing I've ever experienced in my life."

"So based on one childbirth you want to change your entire life?"

Of course he would be skeptical. What else could she expect from him? "Based on one childbirth, several cuts and bruises, a broken leg, a couple of gastrointestinal upsets and a migraine headache, yes, I want to change my life."

"Dr Makela has nothing to do with these feelings? The man loves you. It was obvious in his eyes that day we met in the hall. And you love him, too, don't you? That's the reason for all your sadness?"

Grant had everything to do with her feelings. Now, and always. It was because of Grant that medicine had come alive for her. But thinking that she had any kind of a future with him…it was foolish. "He's an amazing man. He taught me to trust myself, to be confident in my medical instincts. He reminded me I had a talent for taking care of my patients."

Walter didn't respond for a moment, and when he finally did, his voice was full of agony. Something Susan had never heard in him. "You're like your mother in that respect. She had that same kind of compassion for people."

This was the first time she remembered him speaking of her mother, and it surprised her. When she had been much younger, and had asked him questions, he'd always changed the subject. Quite quickly, actually. It hadn't taken long until she'd stopped asking as he wouldn't answer, and there had been no one else to ask. No grandparents, aunts or uncles on her mother's side of the family. So, at a very young age, her mother had been lost to her. "My mother?"

"An amazing woman. She was a nurse, Susan. First time I laid eyes on her, I knew…" He paused, swallowed, cleared his throat. "She had a way with her patients like nothing I've ever seen. I always envied her that because, as a doctor, I had a lousy bedside manner, which is why corporate medicine was such a good fit for me. But she was so patient with me, laughed at some of the ridiculous things I did, and at my awkwardness. Best thing I ever did in my life was to marry that woman, and to this day I still can't figure out why she married me."

"I never knew…"

"And I'm sorry for that. I should have told you more, but it was easier…" His voice broke.

"You married a nurse," she said, as the tears trickled down her face. "I never even knew she was a nurse."

He shook his head, his shoulders sinking into a slump. Walter was a man who never slumped. "She was a kind woman, Susan. She had all the humanity and I had none, but she loved me in spite of the way I was, and always teased me that she would rub off on me. She'd always say it didn't matter how long it took to change me, but she would. She called me her work in progress. Then when she died…" He paused, shut his eyes, drew in a ragged, agonized breath. "I always saw me in you, Susan.

Nothing of your mother. Maybe that's the way I raised you to be because seeing her was just too painful, or maybe that's what I wanted to see. I don't know, and I didn't want to analyze it because it made my life much simpler, raising a version of myself. I was like my father, raised to be like him, and that was good enough. And I've always believed that. But when I saw you in Hawaii…it wasn't me I saw in you. It was your mother, her passion for life, her kindness, her humanity. And what you did for the man you loved…the sacrifice you were willing to make to give him everything he wanted…your mother would have done that for me in spite of all my flaws, and I have a great many of them, Susan. A great many.

"What I realize now is that you're nothing like me, and everything your mother would have wanted you to be. And I hope that even with everything we've been through, and are still going through, we can work it out. Believe me, I've never meant to hurt you. But what I've done… I've never known any other way. And I think I was protecting myself from losing you…from losing the last part of your mother I have."

Walter straightened his shoulders, then depressed the button that stopped the elevator, and stepped out. "I think you should follow your heart, Susan. Wherever it takes you." As the doors started to shut, he forced them open one last time. "You don't suppose there will be grandchildren in this for me, do you?"

This time the doors shut, and Susan wasn't quick enough to get them open again. She was crying too hard, swiping at the tears, not sure whether they were tears of pain, anger…or a little of each. It didn't matter, though. What her father had said…he'd told her to follow her heart. The tears for that were pure joy.

The problem was, she could follow, but when her heart led her back to Grant, what would he do?

* * *

"You'll live," Grant pronounced, putting a bandage on the young man's cut. Good size, about two inches in length, capping off, at an angle, his left eyebrow. The wound required stitches, but he used glue as it was on the boy's face. Neater that way and, for facial wounds, did a better job. "But you'll have a pretty good scar as a souvenir." A reminder of the day he'd challenged the wave and the wave had won. "Next time, when you fall off, clamp your wrists over your ears and bring your elbows together to protect yourself from injuries like this," he said, then showed the boy the proper technique.

The last time he'd explained this maneuver, it had been to Susan. He'd shown her and they'd… "Stay under water for a few moments to let the board get clear before you come back up." If he sounded grumpy, it's because he was. Everything made him grumpy these days. Normally he didn't take it out on his patients, though. Since that's what he seemed to be doing now, it was time to take a break, go clear his head, get his temper in check. "I'll have one of the nurses come in and instruct you on the proper care of your wound, and when you get back home, have your own doctor take a look." With that, he practically flew out of the tiny emergency room, right through the doors and straight to the yard outside. Then, without a thought, he hopped into his Jeep and spun his tires down the dirt road to get away from there.

This last month had been hell in a lot of ways. There had been subtle changes in procedure, nothing that amounted to much—new paperwork, different medicines to try, different equipment. To be honest, the changes were so few it surprised him, and in some ways they were pretty good. Oh, he'd been told that for now Kahawaii would basically be left alone. Which he didn't believe. Promises like that, made at the front end of a new business deal, were rarely kept, so he expected the changes to filter in gradually over time. But for now it was fine.

Except he missed Susan. Missed her like crazy. He'd spent a month trying to hate her for being a Ridgeway, trying to hate her for being like Alana. That would have made things easier. Except she wasn't Alana, and being a Ridgeway was nothing to hate her for. She'd had no say over being born into a large medical corporation, just like he'd had no say about being born to a poor Hawaiian mother. Somehow, those things made each of them who they were and, like it or not, he'd fallen in love with the Ridgeway part of Susan as much as he had every other part.

Well, he'd made a mess of something good, hadn't he? Calling her a distraction, a bad decision. He couldn't blame her for refusing to take his phone calls this past month. He'd left messages, and hoped, but he hadn't been surprised when his attempts to talk to her had been ignored. He deserved that, he thought to himself as he sped up the road to 'Aka 'Aka Falls.

Halfway there he remembered. The last time he'd gone to the falls had been with Susan. Damn it all over again. He couldn't go anywhere, do anything without the memories flooding back.

She approached the falls with trepidation. This wasn't an easy thing to do. She hadn't spoken with Grant in the past month. In fact, she'd gone so far as to refuse his phone calls, which had been for the best. At least it had been when she'd been trying to turn that whole debacle into a strict professional relationship much like she would have with any of the doctors working for Ridgeway Medical.

But this past month…even burying herself in piles and piles of work hadn't helped. Hadn't distracted her from the glaringly obvious. She'd missed Grant. Then after what her father had told her…

There were still so many things to reconcile with his admissions about her mother, and so many things to ask him. She almost laughed aloud. Here she was, thirty-four years old, with so many holes in her life. No one to fill them but her, though. And it was time she did. However that went, she had a new relationship to explore with her father because he *did* know that if this worked out the way she hoped it would, the way she was planning for, she wouldn't be returning to Ridgeway Medical.

Furthermore, this was what her mother would have done, which gave her an amazing amount of comfort in doing something so risky…risky to her heart. But her mother had done that once, for the man she'd loved. For the first time, Susan realized that theirs would have been an enduring marriage had it had enough time. In ways, it had endured. Her father still clung to the memory. And that's what she wanted. Something to cling to, but something more than a memory.

After she parked her rental car near Grant's Jeep, Susan sat there for a few minutes, debating what she should do. She was actually trying to stall because the closer she got, the more daunting this seemed, simply showing up here and asking him to take her in. What if Grant wanted her? *What if he didn't?* With so much uncertainty swirling around her, one thing was for sure. If Grant would have her, Susan Ridgeway Cantwell was on the verge of the biggest change of her life and she was not in control right at this moment, she was so nervous about it. That alone made turning back seem like the most sensible thing to do. But falling in love wasn't always about doing something sensible, was it? And no matter what else happened, in the end, if he still didn't want her…

It was time to be spontaneous, time to quit being stodgy. Time to believe that she deserved to have what she truly wanted. That she *could* have what she wanted.

The jingle of her cell phone interrupted her thoughts. Another call from her father, wanting to know what she was going to do. He'd called about a dozen times since she'd last seen him yesterday, even though he knew she had no idea what was going to happen. She understood that he was anxious about this, but…

"Look, you don't need to keep calling me," she said, as she answered the call. "I'll let you know once I know myself. But so far nothing's happened. I haven't even seen him."

"Know what?" the voice on the other end asked. "Seen who?"

Susan sucked in a sharp breath. "Grant?" she whispered, her voice going immediately shaky.

"Don't hang up," he said immediately.

She wouldn't. Anyone who would come thousands of miles to see the man wouldn't hang up on him, but he didn't know that. Didn't know she was there either. "I won't," she promised.

He didn't say anything for another minute, but she could hear him breathing into the phone. And she couldn't find words to fill in the void. All she knew was that her heart was beating so hard she was about to get light-headed.

So, finally, after an eternity, Grant was the one to begin. "Look, Susan, this is difficult. I've spent this past month trying to figure out what we could do. I mean, what's the proper protocol for a man who's in love with his boss, and there's no way their two worlds can come together?"

"I'm not your boss, Grant."

"You own the clinic I run. Maybe in your world that isn't the same thing as being my boss, but in my world it is."

He didn't sound angry. Which was encouraging. But he didn't sound his usual, casual self either. Which was frightening. "Is it always about two different worlds?" she asked, sensing this could be leading up to the worst possible outcome.

"It shouldn't be," he said honestly. "And I'd like to think that it wouldn't be. But I don't know. You're the one who has lived in both, so you tell me."

She climbed out of her car, and started down the trail to the waterfall, and the pool. She wanted to see him, even if it was to be for the last time. "I know you don't believe me, but I honestly didn't want Kahawaii Clinic to be involved in what we had between us. I thought I'd stumbled into a perfect medical situation in an area that desperately needed it to be what it was, and I truly wanted to work there, to be a part of the kind of medicine you practiced. To me, it wasn't about your world or mine, but about something I was looking for. And I was looking so hard, Grant. I didn't know for what, but I needed something. My position with Ridgeway…it isn't exactly fulfilling. Hasn't been for a while, and not on the level I've wanted it to be.

"I'd been going back and forth, struggling over what to do about it for quite some time now, which was why I ended up where I was…on that beach. I was running away." As she struggled over the terrain, this time she didn't stop to admire the flowers or birds. All she wanted was to see Grant, yet when she stepped into the spot where all she had to do was push back the bushes to reveal it all to her, she couldn't. Such a simple thing and she couldn't bring herself to do it. "I was always honest with you, and that's the best I could do. But you saw me as another Alana, someone who was out to take away everything you loved."

"Maybe I did. At first. When you're losing everything you've planned for most of your life, you can convince yourself of just about anything. But in my heart I knew you weren't like her, Susan, and I've always known that you didn't want to destroy Kahawaii Clinic."

Temptation got the better of her, and Susan finally peeked through the bushes, scanning the entire area of the pool, where she thought he'd be. She didn't see him, though. Didn't see him up on the cliffs either. "But there's the reality of my world to deal with, Grant. I am part owner of Ridgeway Medical, and that's something that won't change, no matter what we work out between us…if you want to work something out between us." She hoped…prayed he would. But if he didn't, she wasn't going to tell herself this was probably for the best, because it wasn't. This was what she wanted. Grant was what she wanted. And the pain already starting its clutch at her heart for fear that he didn't want her wasn't going to go away for a long, long time. If ever.

"I do, Susan," he finally said. "I have this whole time, but when I've been angry…and I've had a lot of angry moments…it was easier to blame rather than trust. Through it all I think I always knew that it was easier to trust rather than blame, *and I did trust you,* even though I wasn't always very good at letting you know. I said hurtful things because I was hurt…"

He stepped up behind her and pulled her into his arms. "But I fell a little in love with you when I watched you fight so hard to save Ryan Harris, and since then my feelings for you have grown."

She melted into his embrace, her back to him, too afraid to turn around. "You wouldn't have if you'd known I was a Ridgeway."

"Then I'd have been stupid," he said. "And in a life filled with so many mistakes, that would have been the worst."

His words brought back the familiar gooseflesh, and she sucked in a sharp breath, then finally spun around to face him. "How did you know I was here?"

He smiled. "How did *you* know I was here?"

"You weren't at the clinic, weren't in your cottage. You said this is where you came to work out your problems… But how did you know?"

"Your father called me."

"He did?" That surprised her.

He nodded. "He said I'd better be good to his daughter. I asked him what that meant, and he said I'd find out soon enough."

"Grant, I've had so many things to think about, to face. To reconsider. And this…this whatever it is between us is so complicated."

"This whatever it is?" he asked. "I've thought it was falling in love."

"With extenuating circumstances. It's so…difficult."

"What part?" he asked. "The part where I love you or the part where you love me?"

"You see, that's just it. Nothing can ever be that simple. I can't *only* be that woman on the beach with the hideous hat, and you can't *only* be the guy on the beach with the incredible surfboard. Nice life if you can get it, but we can't get it, Grant. It's not in my makeup. Not in yours either, except for a few minutes a day."

"So the complications win? The extenuating circumstances beat us? Is that how it's going to end? You can't be the woman in the hat so there's nothing else?" He pulled her even closer. "That's not the Susan Ridgeway I know. She's a real fighter." He chuckled. "And I wouldn't have bought a plane ticket to Dallas to go and see someone who wasn't a fighter."

"You did? You bought a ticket?"

"Leaving day after tomorrow. I couldn't stand it any more. I had to see you. Had to find out if there was anything left between us and figure out a way to work it out if there was."

"I couldn't talk to you, Grant," she said. "I didn't want to be the turmoil that caused you any more problems at Kahawaii. After I questioned you about the way you ran your medical practice, and you showed me the answers…showed me so clearly through your patients…I became your truest believer, so I didn't want to disrupt that, which was why I took myself out of the daily workings of all our Hawaiian facilities. I didn't want to jeopardize anything you do, in any way." And because being involved hurt so deeply it rendered her virtually dysfunctional.

She shut her phone and jammed it in her pocket. "It devastated me when I realized that Kahawaii was part of the deal we were making. I knew that was a horrible decision, not for Ridgeway but for Kahawaii. And after you challenged me to work here…" She looked up, trying to read his face, his eyes, but she couldn't. He didn't frown, didn't smile. There was no sparkle in his eyes, yet no anger there either. What she saw was the seriousness of their world come down to this place, here and now. "What you've got to understand is I wanted to get away from everything I was. From my life, my father, our corporation. I didn't want to remind myself of any of that because I didn't want it to ruin my few days of holiday. I was fooling myself. That's how bad it was for me. And everything you have here…it was so far away, and so vastly different from my life. Then there was you… There was never a moment that I didn't think I would go back to being what I was…until I met you. Until I worked at Kahawaii. Until I fell in love with you. But you were so opposed to us. Admitting that you cared, and even loved me, then telling me it couldn't work out. I even said I'd change, that I'd put an end to everything that complicated us, but you rejected that."

Grant took hold of Susan's hand and pulled her through the bushes into a clearing, where they sat down on the rocks by the pool. "But there's a reality we have to face, Susan," he finally said. "And it is our different worlds. I wanted to ask you to give up everything you are and stay here with me, but that wasn't fair to you. And maybe I thought if I did that, you'd ask me to do the same, which I can't. Then you'd think it was because I didn't love you enough, that loving you wasn't worth the sacrifices I'd have to make. But that was never it. Yet I didn't know how to make it right, because for you to offer it, and for me not to accept, seemed so selfish of me. Then there was Alana, and how stupid I'd been with her. I was afraid…"

"You're not a selfish man, Grant. I know that. And I understand why you couldn't just move to Texas to be with me, or let me buy you the clinic. I think I wouldn't have loved you as much if you had, because that dedication in you for what you have here is so much a part of what I fell in love with, and either way would have been too much of a compromise. And as for Alana, we all make mistakes. I did when I married the wrong man. I did again when I allowed my father to dictate my life. But I really believe that our mistakes can make us better, if we let them."

"If we learn from them."

"We learn, Grant. Sometimes we're too stubborn to admit it, but we do learn." In hard, painful ways sometimes. But ultimately those mistakes would make them better people. She did believe that because she believed in Grant.

"Kekoa," he said.

"Not right now. I think I'm anything but brave right now."

"You came here to work in the clinic, didn't you? To give up everything to work here in the clinic?"

She nodded. "To be with you. And to work as a doctor. A regular staff doctor, if the director will have me."

"He'll have you." He tucked his thumb under her chin and tilted her face toward his. "And in doing that you'll be giving up your corporate job, and everything you know. That's brave, Susan."

"You say brave, but I'm scared."

"Of what?"

"That you won't want me, or that I won't be good enough

as a practicing doctor. It's all so different for me. Things I've never thought I'd do. Things I've never thought I would have." Scared, too, that her father would go back on his promise and turn Kahawaii into something it should never be. She trusted him, but he was still a businessman and different situations precipitated changes in agreements. She had her father's word, but what she had to rely on more than that was Grant.

"Want to know what else is different?" he asked.

His eyes were twinkling now. So much so, she was curious. "What?"

"For starters, you're only going to be my boss for another week or so."

Now she was *really* curious. "How's that?"

"That phone call from your father…when he warned me that you were coming back, he also warned me to be good to his daughter, and to take care of her. And to make her happy."

"And you said…"

"I said that I would dedicate my life to it."

"And he said…"

"That he knew a part of your happiness was tied up in the clinic. He couldn't understand why, and he didn't particularly approve, but it's what Constance would have done. Something about her humanity finally rubbing off in him. He didn't explain what he meant by that."

"My mother," Susan whispered. She would tell Grant the rest some other time. "So, what did he say after that?"

"It wasn't so much what he said as what he did."

Susan held her breath, not sure where this was going.

"He sold me the clinic."

"How?" she sputtered.

"Well, the first thing I did was ask him."

"You asked him to sell you the clinic? You just…asked?"

He nodded. "It's a pretty simple business deal, actually. It involves combining the salary I'm making as a Ridgeway clinic director—which is about ten times more than I was earning before, did you know that?—with another Ridgeway salary… one for a practicing staff physician. I told him that I figured the debt could be paid off in about five years, at which time he'll turn the deed over. Until that time the clinic will still be operated by Ridgeway Medical under the terms by which it currently operates. Of course, that agreement includes only the clinic and a small piece of property. Ridgeway Medical will hang on to the rest of the property for future development because that's where the real monetary value is in all this. All this is contingent on my finding another doctor who wants to partner with me in the venture, as my salary alone won't do it."

"You made that deal?" She smiled, still a bit awestruck.

"I know it's not as complicated as the deals you're used to, but it was the best I could do." A boyish grin crossed his face. "Not bad for someone inexperienced in business negotiations, as your father accepted my offer."

"I can't believe he's selling you Kahawaii."

"Because he loves you. And, actually, he's selling *us* Kahawaii. You and me, Kekoa. Together. And we've got to earn the money as practicing physicians. That was part of my terms to your father, too."

The only way she'd have it. She loved him even more for his integrity in this. "But there's still the matter of my…wealth. I can't deny it, Grant. I want to earn this clinic *with* you, make it ours more than you can know, but that still doesn't change the fact that I'm a Ridgeway, and certain things go along with that, like responsibilities to the corporation, even if I'm not employed there in my previous capacity. I'll have to travel to Texas from time to time, participate in meetings, make decisions. But only on a part-time basis, and not very often. Does that matter to you? Because that's one thing I can't change about myself. I'm a Ridgeway, and if we have children, they'll be Ridgeways, too. I mean, if you want to have children."

"Whoa." He laughed, reaching out to take her hand. "Slow down. From the sound of it, you've given that a lot of thought but, trust me, I'm not one of those men who cares if his wife is wealthy and he's not. I don't care about your investment portfolio, what you have in the bank, anything like that. And if you have to go to Texas from time to time, I'll miss you."

"Well, it's a good thing because, like I said, I come as part owner of Ridgeway Medical, no matter what. And someday it will *all* be mine. Something I'll have to deal with some time, and also something I'll leave to any children I might…we might have. I can't help that."

"How many?" he asked.

"How many what? Dollars do I have?"

He shook his head. "Children do you want? I'm partial to large families, given that neither of us have them."

"I…I'd never thought…" She paused, smiled. "Are you sure about this, Grant? Sure you want to commit to a future with so many Ridgeways?"

His voice went gentle. "Susan, I love you. And there's nothing I want more than to spend the rest of my life with you. But I can't leave here. I can't help that as much as you can't help owning Ridgeway Medical or being a Ridgeway. Those are two insurmountable facts of life we both have to face in order to be together, but we can face them as long as we know what they are and we do it together. So my question to you is, are you sure you want to commit to a future here? Because it won't be anything like you've had."

"I understand that, Grant. And honor it. You shouldn't leave here, and I don't want you to. You need to be here, and so do I. *Me here, with you.* That's what I want…a life *here,* however it comes, practicing medicine at Kahawaii. Living in your cottage, buying the clinic together. Just the two of us on the beach from time to time. Simple things."

"Make sure about this, Susan, because Ridgeway Medical—"

"Will get along fine without me. My father may groan a little about replacing me, but he knows I'm like my mother, and he respects that. So I'm in, Grant. Now, and for ever. There's nothing else. Well, except for one thing."

He gave her a quizzical look.

"It's 'Eleu. She needs a family. She still has her grandfather, and she'll spend time with him when she can, but she needs someone else when she can't be with him. She needs…"

"Us," Grant said. "I've made arrangement for her grandfather to be transferred to a facility not too far from here, a nice place in Kane'ohe. He'll have good care, and they do allow family members to stay there for short visits, so who knows how he'll progress? We'll just have to wait and see. And in the meantime we can add a room to my cottage for her." He started to bend to kiss her, then paused. "You don't mind living in my cottage, do you? Because that's all we're going to have for a while."

"I'd love living in your cottage. And maybe while we're adding on one room for 'Eleu, we should go ahead and add another."

"Another?"

She nodded. "Just in case. After what I have planned for tonight, we may need it." Bracing herself with a deep breath, she said the words she'd been practicing for hours. *"Ko aloha makamae e iop. E hoomau maua kealoha. Ka honi mai me ke aloha." Sweetheart, you are so precious. May our love last for ever. And with that love is a kiss.*

Touched by her words, Grant kissed her, long and deep. *"Mau loa. Me ke aloha no kau a kau,"* he replied when it ended. *For ever. My love, for eternity.* "And are you sure you want to wait until tonight? I've heard that many miracles have begun at 'Aka 'Aka Falls."

For her, it had begun that first day she'd come to the beach and watched the most beautiful man in the world enter the water with his surfboard. She looked forward to that in the years to come—going to the beach, watching the man she loved, collecting a few shells. "I've had my miracle," she said. "But I'm certainly willing to try for another one." She snaked an arm around his neck. "Want to be a little more specific about the nature of that miracle at 'Aka 'Aka Falls?"

"Well, first it starts with a swim."

She smiled, pleased with the suggestion, as she began to unbutton her blouse. "This time, can we swim naked?"

008/02

MILLS & BOON
*Romance*

## On sale 7th November 2008

*Get into the Christmas spirit this month as*
*Mills & Boon® Romance brings you...*

### WEDDED IN A WHIRLWIND *by Liz Fielding*

Miranda is on a dream tropical island holiday when disaster
strikes! She's stranded in a dark cave...and she's not alone.
Miranda is trapped with macho adventurer Nick – and the
real adventure is just about to begin...

### BLIND DATE WITH THE BOSS *by Barbara Hannay*

Sally has come to Sydney for a fresh start. And she's trying
to ignore her attraction to her brooding boss, Logan.
Fun-loving Sally has waltzed into Logan's life and it will
never be the same again...

### THE TYCOON'S CHRISTMAS PROPOSAL
*by Jackie Braun*

With the dreaded holidays approaching, the last thing widowed
businessman Dawson needs is a personal shopper who wants to
get *personal*. Eve is determined that the festive fun begins!

### CHRISTMAS WISHES, MISTLETOE KISSES
*by Fiona Harper*

Louise is determined to make this Christmas perfect for her and
her young son. But it's not until she meets gorgeous architect
Ben that her Christmas really begins to sparkle...

*Available at WHSmith, Tesco, ASDA, and all good bookshops*
*www.millsandboon.co.uk*

MILLS & BOON
# MEDICAL
## On sale 7th November 2008

### DR DEVEREUX'S PROPOSAL
*by Margaret McDonagh*

### BRIDES OF PENHALLY BAY
*Bachelor doctors become husbands and fathers –
in a place where hearts are made whole*

It's the sexy French accent that captures Lauren's attention –
before she's even seen Penhally Bay's gorgeous new doctor!
Lauren is overawed by Dr Gabe Devereux's attention, but, with
her sight declining, is vulnerable Lauren willing to let Gabe
be her only guiding light...forever?

### CHILDREN'S DOCTOR, MEANT-TO-BE WIFE
*by Meredith Webber*

When an unknown virus emerges at Crocodile Creek kids' camp,
Beth Stuart knows the only person to call is her ex-husband,
he's the best in his field. As they work together, their love and
passion rekindle, making Angus realise he has to convince
Beth to give them another chance.

### ITALIAN DOCTOR, SLEIGH-BELL BRIDE
*by Sarah Morgan*

Nurse Liv Winchester has avoided men since her ex left her
with a baby. Yet new trauma consultant Stefano Lucarelli
makes this overworked mum feel like a beautiful woman again.
Stefano, however, needs more than magical dates and
expensive gifts to persuade Liv that she's ready to
be his bride for real...

Available at WHSmith, Tesco, ASDA, and all good bookshops
www.millsandboon.co.uk

1008/03b

MILLS & BOON

# MEDICAL

## On sale 7th November 2008

### CHRISTMAS AT WILLOWMERE
#### by Abigail Gordon

The Cheshire village of Willowmere sparkles as Christmas approaches – and there's an early surprise when gorgeous Dr Glenn Hamilton re-enters practice nurse Anna Bartlett's life! Though he warms her heart, she knows there can be no future for them – Glenn is determined to find out why she's holding back...

### DR ROMANO'S CHRISTMAS BABY
#### by Amy Andrews

Nurse Rilla Winters is shocked that the new A&E doctor at Brisbane General is...her husband! It's been years since they parted, and Luca Romano's reappearance, in all his Italian glory, throws her into confusion. With emotions riding high, they spend one special night together – and Rilla falls pregnant...

### THE DESERT SURGEON'S SECRET SON
#### by Olivia Gates

Seven years ago sheikh and surgeon Ghaleb Aal Omraan chose duty over love, leaving Viv LaSalle broken-hearted – and, unknowingly, pregnant. Stunned that his new Director of Surgery is Viv, Ghaleb finds their passion stronger than ever. With his state marriage imminent, Viv knows she must escape before Ghaleb discovers his son!

Available at WHSmith, Tesco, ASDA, and all good bookshops
www.millsandboon.co.uk

# *Celebrate 100 years of pure reading pleasure with Mills & Boon®*

To mark our centenary, each month we're publishing a special 100th Birthday Edition. These celebratory editions are packed with extra features and include a FREE bonus story.

Plus, you have the chance to enter a fabulous monthly prize draw. See 100th Birthday Edition books for details.

*Now that's worth celebrating!*

### September 2008
**Crazy about her Spanish Boss by Rebecca Winters**
Includes FREE bonus story
*Rafael's Convenient Proposal*

### November 2008
**The Rancher's Christmas Baby
by Cathy Gillen Thacker**
Includes FREE bonus story *Baby's First Christmas*

### December 2008
**One Magical Christmas by Carol Marinelli**
Includes FREE bonus story *Emergency at Bayside*

Look for Mills & Boon® 100th Birthday Editions at your favourite bookseller or visit
www.millsandboon.co.uk

LAXY_AD

# Lose yourself
### in a good
### book with Galaxy

Curled up on the sofa,
Sunday morning in pyjamas,
just before bed,
in the bath or
on the way to work?

Wherever, whenever,
you can escape
with a good book!

So go on...
indulge yourself with
a good read and the
smooth taste of
Galaxy chocolate

*Proud Sponsors of The British Book Awards*

Galaxy
British**BOOK**
AWARDS
2008

# 4 FREE

## BOOKS AND A SURPRISE GIFT!

We would like to take this opportunity to thank you for reading this Mills & Boon® book by offering you the chance to take FOUR more specially selected titles from the Medical™ series absolutely FREE! We're also making this offer to introduce you to the benefits of the Mills & Boon® Book Club—

- ★ **FREE home delivery**
- ★ **FREE gifts and competitions**
- ★ **FREE monthly Newsletter**
- ★ **Exclusive Mills & Boon® Book Club offers**
- ★ **Books available before they're in the shops**

Accepting these FREE books and gift places you under no obligation to buy, you may cancel at any time, even after receiving your free shipment. Simply complete your details below and return the entire page to the address below. You don't even need a stamp!

**YES!** Please send me 4 free Medical books and a surprise gift. I understand that unless you hear from me, I will receive 6 superb new titles every month for just £2.99 each, postage and packing free. I am under no obligation to purchase any books and may cancel my subscription at any time. The free books and gift will be mine to keep in any case.

M8ZED

Ms/Mrs/Miss/Mr .............................................Initials .........................................

BLOCK CAPITALS PLEASE

Surname ....................................................................................................................

Address ....................................................................................................................

.................................................................................................................................

.........................................................................Postcode.........................................

**Send this whole page to:**
**UK: FREEPOST CN81, Croydon, CR9 3WZ**

Offer valid in UK only and is not available to current Mills & Boon® Book Club subscribers to this series. Overseas and Eire please write for details and readers in Southern Africa write to Box 3010, Pinegowie, 2123 RSA. We reserve the right to refuse an application and applicants must be aged 18 years or over. Only one application per household. Terms and prices subject to change without notice. Offer expires 31st December 2008. As a result of this application, you may receive offers from Harlequin Mills & Boon and other carefully selected companies. If you would prefer not to share in this opportunity please write to The Data Manager, PO Box 676, Richmond, TW9 1WU.

Mills & Boon® is a registered trademark owned by Harlequin Mills & Boon Limited.
Medical™ is being used as a trademark. The Mills & Boon® Book Club is being used as a trademark.